Praise for
my Basmati
Bat Mitzvah

★ "The latest spunky heroine of South Asian–Jewish heritage
to grace middle-grade fiction, Tara Feinstein, 12, charms readers
from the get-go in this strong, funny debut."
—Kirkus Reviews, starred review

"Tara's inquisitiveness, openness, and determination
to chart her own path stand out in this warm story of family,
faith, and the ways people are unique yet intertwined."
—Publishers Weekly

"With a conversational and authentic tween voice, Tara invites readers
into her world. . . . Her questions regarding God are poignant and relatable
while her opinions on training bras are simply spot-on."
—Bulletin of the Center for Children's Books

"Authors often mention but then shrink from exploring
in depth their characters' mixed religious heritage. . . . Freedman
bucks that trend, avoiding didacticism by portraying broader issues
through Tara's personality and unique circumstances."
—Jewish Daily Forward

"This story will have resonance for many children
of many faiths at the cusp of religious adulthood."
—Booklist

AMULET BOOKS
NEW YORK

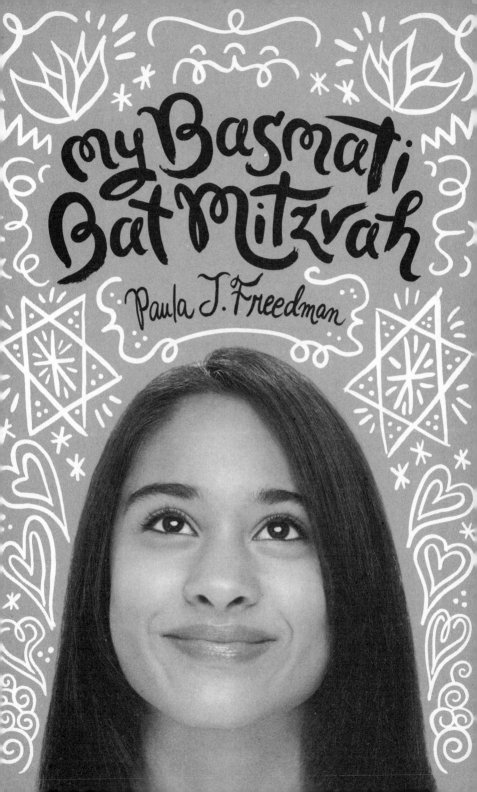

my Basmati
Bat Mitzvah

Paula J. Freedman

The Library of Congress has catalogued the hardcover edition of this book as follows:

Freedman, Paula J.
My basmati bat mitzvah / Paula J. Freedman.
pages cm
Summary: Tara Feinstein, proud of both her East Indian and Jewish heritage, ponders what it means to have a bat mitzvah and deals with her own questions about her faith.
ISBN 978-1-4197-0806-0 (alk. paper)
[1. Bat mitzvah—Fiction. 2. Judaism—Fiction.
3. Jews—United States—Fiction.
4. East Indian Americans—Fiction.] I. Title.
PZ7.F87286My 2013
[Fic]—dc23
2013005791

ISBN for this edition: 978-1-4197-1368-2

Text copyright © 2013 Paula J. Freedman
Book design by Sara Corbett

Printed and bound in U.S.A.
10 9 8 7 6 5 4 3 2 1

Amulet Books are available at special discounts when purchased in quantity for premiums and promotions as well as fundraising or educational use. Special editions can also be created to specification. For details, contact specialsales@abramsbooks.com or the address below.

ABRAMS
THE ART OF BOOKS SINCE 1949
115 West 18th Street
New York, NY 10011
www.amuletbooks.com

This book is dedicated to Kulbir;
to the memory of my father, Howard Freedman;
and to the rest of my *desi mishpacha*,
with love.

Chapter 1

When Ben-o came over on Saturday for movie night, my dad answered the door wearing gray silk pajama bottoms and his *Math Teachers Play by the Numbers* T-shirt, an unlit pipe clenched between his teeth.

"Ben-o, old chap!" he cried heartily. "How are you, dear boy?"

Daddy was practicing his Jay Gatsby routine—so embarrassing. His eleventh-graders were reading *The Great Gatsby* in their English class, so he planned to go to school on Monday in character—even though he teaches math, not English. I hoped it wouldn't turn into a phase, like last year, which was much worse—steampunk. At least he doesn't go around wearing a leather helmet and aviator goggles anymore.

"Good, Mr. Feinstein."

"Joshua, Ben-o, pal," Daddy said, slapping him on the back. "Call me Joshua."

I wished he wouldn't call him Ben-o. It sounded stupid when he said it. Ben-o started being called Ben-o because of the other Ben—Ben D.—who moved away in fourth grade. But Daddy didn't even know that.

Ben O'Connell is like my best friend in the whole world, besides Rebecca. He lives three floors down, so we practically grew up together. He didn't even put on shoes to come upstairs.

I stood across the room, next to Mum, watching with embarrassment. Daddy teaches trigonometry and calculus. He is, by definition, not cool, but he tries to compensate by getting into whatever "all the kids" are into. Which is double uncool, but his students love him. Mum, on the other hand, doesn't even try to be cool. It's one of her more endearing qualities.

"Tara," she said, "go and rescue Benjamin from your father." She gave me a not-so-subtle push forward, sending me not-so-gracefully bounding across the room. "Come along, Joshua," she added.

"Hey," I said when they left.

"Hey," Ben-o said.

I looked him up and down, puzzled. "Why are you dressed like that?"

He was wearing a red polo shirt, tucked into a pair of jeans with no obvious holes in them. Something was up with his hair, too, but I couldn't quite put my finger on it.

His face flushed all the way up to his ears.

"Like what?" he asked, trying to sound casual.

"Like—since when do you tuck in?"

Ben-o surveyed himself in surprise, as if his shirt had tucked itself in when he wasn't looking. He shrugged.

"Never mind," I said. "You look nice, is all."

"Um, thanks," he mumbled.

We went to the kitchen then and made two bags of microwave popcorn. I covered mine with *chaat masala*, an addictive mix of Indian dry spices made especially for snacks, but Ben-o just had salt on his, because *masala* powder makes him cough.

No kidding, India has the best salty snacks in the world. Nothing we have in the West compares, not potato chips or pretzels or even nachos. I've never understood why Americans are so crazy for Mexican food but not Indian. The secret Indian snack-food ingredient is mango powder, which is Hindi for "that which makes everything taste delicious." Between that and the black sea salt, once you start eating it, you can't stop.

I get my snacketite from Nanaji—my Indian grandfather. His favorites included *chana jor garam*, whole chickpeas mashed flat, fried, and seasoned with *chaat masala*. *Golgappas*, crisp pastry globes filled with a spicy liquid that you had to pop in your mouth whole. Crunchy *bhel puri*. Steaming samosas. Savory *aloo tikki* patties. Then there were the sweets.

"Once you have tasted proper *kulfi*," Nanaji used to say, dreamily, "you will forget your ice cream."

Ben-o had brought over his whole binder of horror-movie DVDs. We agreed on *Bloody Fools*, a goofy vampire story where everyone talks in fake British accents.

He slouched down next to me on the couch, fiddling with the remote. I reached over and touched his hair. When we were little, he used to let me braid it or gather it up into a ponytail and then spring it free. I loved the way his hair, if you stretched it, was long and silky, and then you let go and it *sproinged* back into place. You wouldn't have guessed how long it really was unless we went swimming at the Y and he was just coming out of a dive off the high board and it was all plastered back and reaching past his shoulders. One shake and the curls would bounce back into place.

Today it felt different. Coarse. Not curly.

"Why's it all fluffy?"

"That happens when I comb it."

"You can't comb curly hair! Even I know that," I said. "You have to just let it go natural. Or cut it all off." Boys can be so clueless.

Whoosh. I saw his right ear and cheek go red again.

I wondered what was up with him lately. Combing his hair, tucking in shirts—the week before, he'd brought over flowers for Mum, from his mom's rooftop garden.

The movie started, and we both shrieked in pretend-terror when the first vampire, Joffrey, jumped out from behind the fake boulder—as if we hadn't seen it like a hundred times. We clutched hands, laughing and shivering.

But then Daddy came in with some tall iced teas, and Ben-o dropped my hand and scooted to the other side of the couch. Daddy put the tray down on the ottoman and sat in the adjacent armchair.

"I say, old sports. Whatcha watching?"

"*Bloody Fools*," Ben-o mumbled, taking an iced tea from the tray.

"Beg pardon?"

"That's the name of the movie," I said.

"I hope it's not rated R," Daddy said. "Let me see the box."

"Daddy! We've seen this movie like a hundred times."

"We have?"

"Not you—me and Ben-o."

He watched with us for like ten minutes, totally ruining the mood, especially because he kept laughing at how dumb the movie was. Which was true, but that was sort of the point. When Daddy wasn't looking, Ben-o did a fake stretch and draped his arm over the back of the couch, around my shoulders. Which was totally weird, especially with my dad sitting there, alternately chomping on an unlit pipe and loud-slurping an iced tea. I started to giggle. If Ben-o's move was a joke, I didn't quite get it, but I laughed as if I did. I felt his arm stiffen, but he didn't move it.

Mum poked her head around the corner. "Joshua," she said, motioning with her eyebrows that he should join her in the other room, but Daddy remained oblivious.

"What?" he said.

"Leave. The kids. Alone."

"Oh, right," he said, standing up. Then he added, without even looking, "Both hands where I can see them, O'Connell." Ben-o dropped his arm.

After that, he didn't try to put his arm around me again and I didn't play with his hair. We just watched the movie, laughing at all the best parts and imitating the actors' terrible accents.

"Jolly good," we told each other when it ended.

"Yes, smashing."

"Brilliant, what?"

Ben-o lapsed back into silence after we'd run through our repertoire of undead-Englishman impressions. He started messing with his hair. I regretted saying anything about it, but honestly, what was up with him lately? He never used to care when I teased him. Or not know what to say. Finally, I asked, "Do you want to watch another one?"

"Nah," he said.

"Want to play a game?"

"Sure."

I fished out two controllers from the cabinet under the TV and handed him one. I popped in Stingray Rampage without even asking, since we're pretty evenly matched in that one.

He seemed to be more comfortable now that we were facing the screen instead of each other.

"Who'd you get for homeroom?" he asked.

I made a face, even though he couldn't see. "Ross," I said. "You?"

"Heinrich."

"So jelly," I said, demolishing an alien. Mr. H is our science teacher and the adviser for Robotics Club. He's probably my favorite teacher ever. I have a tiny crush on him because he wears short-sleeve plaid shirts and enormous black-rimmed glasses and I like the way his hair sticks up in the back when he's writing on the board. "Oh, and—Rebecca's walking with us on Monday. She doesn't have basketball until next week."

"Hey," Ben-o said, "want to join the chess club this year? It's on Tuesdays after school."

"Can't," I said. "Hebrew school."

"Oh, right," he said. "This is your last year, though, right?"

"Yeah," I said, thinking, *Next year I'm gonna have to come up with a different excuse.* I really didn't get the appeal of competition chess. But if I said that out loud, I would get a full-on strategy lecture from Ben-o.

"When is your thing?" Ben-o asked, meaning my bat mitzvah.

"December," I said. "If I go through with it."

"Like you have a choice?"

"Of course." When Mum enrolled me in Hebrew school two years ago, I was skeptical—for one thing, the other kids had already been going for three years, so I had a lot of catching up to do—but we all agreed to keep an open mind. "You can't force someone to have a bat mitzvah," I told Ben-o. "Like—they have to believe in God and stuff." At least, I assumed that was true.

Whether or not *I* believed in God—that was the main question. I had thought about it all summer, and I still didn't know the answer. There wasn't even anyone I could talk to about it. I mean—it wasn't exactly something you wanted to ask your rabbi. Rabbi Aron is probably the coolest rabbi in the world, but still. My heart did a flip just thinking about that conversation: *"Um, Rabbi? I have this friend who maybe doesn't believe in God . . . Can I—I mean, she—I mean, he . . ."* See? Scary.

"Well, I don't have a choice about my confirmation," Ben-o said. "Not that I'm against it."

"Hmm," I said, which is what I say when I don't want to argue. Not being against something isn't the same as being for something. Having a confirmation or a bat mitzvah is a big deal. A commitment. Not a decision to be taken lightly. Or just because everyone else is doing it.

"Aren't you a little bit worried, though?" he asked after a while.

"About what?"

"Like, if you don't have one—that you might go to hell or something."

Well, *that* hadn't occurred to me before. I took out three of Ben-o's Stingbats while I considered the question. "I don't think Jews believe in hell," I said.

Ben-o glanced at me, then back at the screen. "Seriously?"

"I don't think we have one."

"That's weird."

"Why's it weird? Maybe believing in hell is weird." For some reason, all this talk about religion was making me feel defensive.

"No, that's cool, only—like, how do you know right from wrong?"

"I just *do*. So do you."

"But maybe that's because I was taught about heaven and hell and stuff."

That made me upset. So Jews not believing in hell meant we couldn't tell right from wrong? What about the other gajillion people on the planet—the Muslims, Buddhists, Hindus, Sikhs, atheists, et cetera? It wasn't like they were going around killing each other all the time.

"No," I said. "I don't believe you. You're a good person, in here." I thumped my chest, taking a hand off the controller. "You're not just pretending to be good because you're afraid of going to hell. You were born good."

Ben-o cringed, then swooped in and captured one of my Stingbats.

"I guess so."

But what if he was right? What if, by not having a bat mitzvah, or by being Jewish instead of Christian, or maybe, just maybe, not believing in God—what if I was doomed? Condemned to some nightmarish eternity? Was that a good enough reason to have a bat mitzvah or, in Ben-o's case, a confirmation? Go through the motions, just in case?

We played in silence then, and without mercy. I got the feeling Ben-o was a little offended. So was I. That felt weird and uncomfortable. We finished a level, and pretty soon after that, Ben-o said he had to go home.

"I'm sorry," I said as he was leaving.

Ben-o smiled. "Don't worry about it," he said, shaking his head. His hair barely moved. "It doesn't matter."

I hoped he was right. But I knew deep down that he wasn't—that it *did* matter, in ways I had tried not to think about before. Like—did my having a bat mitzvah mean that Ben-o and I would have less in common? I hadn't ever thought so before, but I'd also assumed we had the same ideas about right and wrong. Something else was nagging at me, too—nothing to do with Ben-o. It was this: Was I about to become more Jewish, or less Indian? Did making a choice—to do something I wasn't even sure about—mean having to leave Nanaji behind? Because that was never going to happen. Not ever.

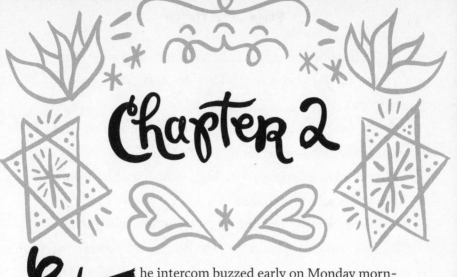

Chapter 2

The intercom buzzed early on Monday morning. It was Sal, the doorman, letting me know Rebecca was on her way up.

"You're early," I said by way of greeting when she came upstairs. I could tell she was nervous about her first-day-of-school outfit, even though she looked the way she always looks—perfect. She dropped her backpack on the floor near the gold-framed mirror in the hall, scowling at her reflection. She stopped, turning to face me.

"You're wearing that today?" she asked, surveying my outfit.

"Uh, yeah," I said. I had spent the entire weekend putting it together, and frankly, I'd nailed it: white tights, vintage blue-and-green plaid school-uniform skirt, black extra-high-top sneaker boots, and one of Daddy's sprung-out old concert tees. "What's wrong with it?"

"Nothing, just—on the first day? I mean, everyone's going to be wearing new clothes."

"These *are* new," I said. Rebecca raised an eyebrow. "New to me, anyway." Rebecca wouldn't be caught dead wearing vintage.

"It looks cool," she admitted, backpedaling now. "But you could have saved it for tomorrow."

"Like I'm gonna wear a Catholic-school skirt to Hebrew school?" I snorted. "Please."

Rebecca busied herself futzing with her stick-straight hair, as if she could ever get it to do anything other than what it wanted. She viciously pushed a strand behind her ear. Then she shifted her focus back to her clothes, experimenting with opening and closing the top button of the striped oxford shirt she wore beneath a brand-new green cashmere sweater. She wrinkled her nose like a bunny, turning her head from side to side, trying to catch her own profile. Mum came out of her office then.

"Don't you look nice, Rebecca. That green sweater suits you. You know, I have a scarf with that exact color running through it . . . Would you like to borrow it? Tara, is that what you're wearing to school?"

"Can I?" Rebecca breathed. I thought she was going to perish with joy right on the spot. Rebecca definitely has a mom-crush on my mother.

I sighed and grabbed Rebecca by the arm, pulling her toward the front door. "Come on," I said. "We're going to be late. You wouldn't want that to happen on the first day, would you? Start the year off with a deficit to your perfect attendance record?"

When we got downstairs, Ben-o was already in the lobby, talking to Sal. Mrs. Donovan, my next-door neighbor, was perched on the bench near the mailboxes, clucking disapprovingly.

"Young man, where are your big-boy shoes?" she demanded.

Ben-o looked down. Once again, he'd tucked his shirt neatly into his pants, but on his feet was a cheap pair of rubber flip-flops. He grinned sheepishly. "Nothing else fits me," he said.

It was true. I'd heard Mrs. O telling Mum that he'd already outgrown the new basketball shoes he got for back-to-school, and how it was too late to bring them back because he'd scuffed them up.

"Don't worry, Mrs. D," he reassured her. "My mom is taking me shopping after school today."

Mrs. D grumbled something about the "crazy stuff" that "kids today" wear, which would never have been tolerated "in my day," and something about "respect for the institution," the "destructive influence of video games," and a "rampant irreverence toward all that is holy." Behind her back, Sal mimicked her fluttery hand gestures and the shocked expression on her face. It was all we could do to keep a straight face.

When we got outside, I saw Sheila Rosenberg up ahead with Missy Abrams—which was odd, because Missy didn't live nearby. But no one wanted to walk into school alone on the first day.

I pretended not to see them. Missy Abrams is all right, but Sheila Rosenberg is a major know-it-all. Last year she told me that my dad could never be buried in a Jewish cemetery because of the *pi* tattoo on his left arm—which he got the year all his seniors passed the AP calculus exam. I told her it didn't matter, because A, he's not dying, and B, both my parents are going to be cremated. I didn't know if that was true, but Nanaji had been cremated, so it popped into my head. Sheila had seemed troubled by this information, but she didn't say anything until Hebrew school, when she actually asked Mrs. Moskowitz if Jews were *allowed* to be cremated! As if it was any of her business.

"Hey, Sheila!" Rebecca yelled now. "Hey, Missy!" They both stopped, smiled, and waved in unison. They waited for us to catch up. Great.

"What are you doing?" I hissed.

"What?" said Rebecca. "I'm just being friendly. God. Sheila's in my homeroom."

I didn't get time to ask her how she knew that.

"Hi, Rebecca," said Sheila. "Hello, Tara. Hello, Ben."

Missy then greeted each of us by name, too.

"Hey, everyone," I said, impatient to move it along.

Ben-o jerked his chin at them and said, "'Sup."

We all compared homerooms. Missy was in Ben-o's, and she said Jenna Alberts was, too. The only person I knew for sure was in my homeroom was Aisha Khan, because Mum and I had bumped into her at the dentist the week before. We'd planned to meet up in front of school at 8:40.

I caught sight of her as we came around the last corner, near the basketball courts. I waved for her to join us.

"Guess who's in our class?" she asked, not even waiting for me to answer. "Ryan Berger."

"Ugh," I said. Ryan Berger is a major goon.

Aisha shrugged. "He's cute," she said.

"He only dates Jewish girls," Sheila observed.

I stared at her with my mouth open. What a rude thing to say.

"She only said he's *cute*," I said. "Not that I agree. No offense, Aisha."

"None taken." Aisha shrugged. "Anyway, it doesn't matter. I'm not allowed to date anyone, ever."

"You mean, like, until high school?" Rebecca asked innocently.

"I mean, like, until I get married," Aisha replied. Rebecca laughed, but I'm pretty sure Aisha wasn't kidding. Her parents are really old-school.

I quickly steered the subject back to Ryan Berger. "Since when does he *date*?" I asked Sheila.

"Well, not literally, but he's only allowed to date Jewish people when he does start dating."

"Then there's hope for you yet, Sheila," I said. Rebecca poked me in the ribs. Ben-o smirked.

✶ ✶ ✶

Ryan Berger was all over me in homeroom. He kept asking me questions, like—"Who'd you get for English?" And I was like, "Galvez—honors class." And then he was like, "Is your friend Rebecca in that class?" And I was like, "Yeah, and P.E. and Social Studies, too." And he was like, "What about Hebrew school?" And I was like, "I don't know yet. We'll find out tomorrow. Why are you asking me so many questions about Rebecca?" And he was like, "No reason. I'm just used to seeing you together." And I was like, "What about Ben-o?" And he was like, "What about him?" And then—"Hey, are you doing any sports this year?" And I was like, "No, but I'm doing Robotics."

After that, thankfully, he turned to Aisha and asked her a couple hundred questions. It turned out they had four classes together. Aisha sighed happily.

Ms. Ross was trying to get everyone to sit down, her high, nasal voice barely audible over the noise of everyone talking and laughing and moving chairs around. Ryan sat down at the desk next to me.

"You can't sit there, Ryan. Aisha and I want to sit together," I said. He got up and moved forward one seat but turned sideways to face me. "Where's *your* sidekick?" I added.

"Why are you obsessing about Adam?" he teased, his hard little eyes glinting.

"I'm not—I'm just not used to seeing you apart."

"He's in Mr. H's homeroom."

"So's Ben-o," I said. "They're lucky."

Ryan shrugged. I turned my head, trying to get a sideways glimpse of him without staring directly. I'd always been fascinated by those eyes—so glittery and hard, you couldn't even tell what color they were. They just reflected back at you, like broken glass. Looking into them made my eyes tear up, but not with emotion. More like an allergy, or staring into a flashlight. You can't trust a person like that.

Ms. Ross distributed some home-information forms she said we had to fill out before the bell rang. Ryan asked Aisha if he could borrow a pen.

"You don't have a pen on the first day of school?" I asked.

"It's okay," Aisha said, fishing one out of her backpack. "You can keep it."

"Thanks," said Ryan, tossing it in the air a few times. Then he missed and it skidded across the room, under the radiator. Ms. Ross wouldn't let him go get it, so he put his head down on the table while the rest of us filled out our forms. He pretended to snore, which made Aisha giggle.

There was a tap at the back door of the classroom, and I looked up to see Ben-o in the hallway, motioning for me to come out. He grinned.

I raised my hand, but Ross was so busy bleating instructions at everyone that she didn't see.

"May I have the hall pass?" I called out. "My stomach hurts."

Ms. Ross is maybe twenty-two years old and looks like she's terrified of kids. Which is understandable, because she's shorter than most of the boys in the seventh grade. She was brand-new last year and had a reputation for sending kids to the principal's office for almost no reason. She was in way over her head.

"I'm finished," I added, waving the form.

Ryan looked up. "Gimme your pen," he mouthed, so I tossed it to him. This time he caught it.

Ms. Ross hesitated, eyeing me with suspicion, but I put on a good show of pretending my stomach hurt, and she relented. She motioned me to her desk and handed me the pass.

"Be back in five minutes," she said.

I slipped out into the hall, where Ben-o was waiting.

"How's Mr. H's class?" I said.

"Awesome," Ben-o said, smiling.

"So lucky. Ross has lost control already."

Ben-o snorted. "How's Berger?"

"Totally annoying. He might have a crush on Rebecca."

"I don't think so," Ben-o said.

"Whatever," I said. "What are you doing out here?"

"I forgot to give you this." He reached into his back pocket and handed me a small book with a fancy teal cover, like cool wallpaper, secured with a silver elastic strap.

"Thanks!" I said. "What is it?"

"It's a datebook—like a planner. Do you like it? I got one, too, in black. Mom says I need to get organized . . . See, you can put your schedule here, and there's a separate place to write down homework assignments."

"Cool," I said. "It's really pretty, too—"

Ben-o blushed.

"—but I didn't get you anything."

"That's okay," Ben-o said. "It wasn't, like, a planned thing. I just saw it and thought you would like it."

"I have to get back now," I said.

"Me, too," Ben-o said. "See you later."

"Yeah."

Since when did Ben-o buy me presents? He was always saving up for something—a remote-controlled helicopter or some electronic gizmo. I mean, probably his mom had paid for this, but still. I went back into the classroom and put the hall pass on Ross's desk.

"What's that?" asked Aisha when I sat down.

"A datebook. Ben-o gave it to me."

"Can I see?" I handed it to her and she flipped through the pages. "This is really cool," she said. "Do you know where he got it?"

I shook my head. "You can ask him at lunch."

"Present from your boyfriend?" Ryan asked, a mocking glint in those hard little eyes.

"He's not my boyfriend," I said.

"Then why'd he get you a *date*book?"

"It's a calendar, stupid."

The bell rang and it was time for a real class—Honors English. With Rebecca. I gathered my things and waved good-bye to Aisha. I didn't wave good-bye to Berger. I didn't even ask for my pen back.

✳ ✳ ✳

Mr. Galvez let us choose our own seats for Honors English, so I got to sit next to Rebecca.

"What's that?" she wanted to know as soon as we sat down.

"My new planner. Ben-o gave it to me."

"Let me see," she demanded, putting out her hand. I didn't mind, because I hadn't written anything in it yet. I handed it to her and she flipped through the pages the way Aisha had. I saw her pause on a page, and then she snapped the book shut.

"Hmm," she said.

"Hmm?" I replied.

"Nothing," she said. "Just, since when does he give you stuff?"

I was wondering the same thing, but I didn't think it was a big deal.

"It's not a big deal," I said.

"Okay," Rebecca said, handing it back to me. She gave me a funny look. "If you say so."

Chapter 3

yan wasn't in homeroom on Tuesday. I found out later that he and Adam Greenspan had already gotten in trouble and weren't allowed to come back without their parents.

After school, Rebecca and I grabbed a snack at her place and ate it on the way over to Hebrew school. We wanted to get there early to find out which class we were in. I guess everyone else had the same idea, because the hallway outside Rabbi's office, where the class rosters were posted, was packed. Rebecca and I were both in Rabbi Aron's class, which was a relief. I'd heard a rumor that only the smart kids got Rabbi Aron for their bar or bat mitzvah year. Judging from the fact that Ryan Berger and Adam Greenspan were in Ms. Jacobson's class, it was probably true. But it also meant prissy Sheila Rosenberg was in Rabbi Aron's with us.

In the middle of all the normal jostling, Ryan came barreling down the hall, pretending to shoot Adam, and Adam pretended to die, clutching his chest and sinking to the floor in a slow, staggering swoon. As he fell, he stepped on my foot and almost knocked Rebecca over.

"Hey, watch it!" I said, catching Adam before he knocked us all over like a bunch of dominoes. "Didn't you two already get suspended?" I couldn't help being a little bit impressed: getting kicked out of middle school for setting off a fart bomb—on the very first day? That was a new record. Too bad their punishment didn't extend to Hebrew school, too.

"My mother is so proud." Ryan sniffed, wiping away a fake tear. Only Adam cracked up. Rebecca rolled her eyes.

The hall was buzzing with first-day excitement, even though it was, um, *Hebrew school*, and everyone was comparing bar and bat mitzvah dates.

Ryan made the mistake of asking Sheila Rosenberg when her "bar mitzvah" was.

"It's *bat* mitzvah," Sheila said, correcting him. "Only boys have *bar* mitzvahs. Don't you know anything after five years of Hebrew?"

"Here we go," I muttered to Rebecca, who just shook her head and looked at Sheila with something like pity.

But Ryan, surprisingly, didn't take the bait, probably because he couldn't think of anything funny to say. Instead he turned to me and Rebecca. I wondered again if he had a crush on her, considering the dumb questions he'd asked me in homeroom on Monday. In a way, I felt sorry for him, because—*Rebecca*? That was never going to happen. Not in a million years. "When are yours?" he asked, looking mainly at me, even though I was pretty sure he meant her.

"Hers is February," I said, pointing to Rebecca. "Mine's in December. Right before Hanukkah"—automatically adding, in my head: *if I go through with it.*

"And when's yours, Ryan?" Rebecca asked, just to be polite. It wasn't like we were going to be invited, or vice versa. She sounded as bored as possible.

"November," Ryan said. "Adam's is in March." Not that anyone asked.

"Mine's the first one," said Sheila. "In October."

"Who cares?" said Ryan.

Sheila shrugged. "You asked."

"That's *soon*," Rebecca said, turning to her. "Are you going to be ready?"

"I already started taking lessons with Rabbi Aron over the summer," Sheila replied, seeming really impressed with herself.

"You went to Hebrew school in the *summer*?" Ryan asked, incredulous. Adam's mouth hung open.

I didn't think that was so weird, actually. I mean, if my bat mitzvah were coming up that soon, and if I were definitely going through with it, I probably would have done the same thing. To tell you the truth, I kind of *liked* Hebrew school, especially the history stuff, like how the Maccabees drove the invaders out of Jerusalem and reclaimed the holy temple. It was cool to read about stuff like that because it definitely really happened. I had a harder time with the Bible stories, though. I mean, Jonah gets swallowed by a whale—and lives to tell about it? Really?

Not that Hebrew school was easy. For one thing, Hebrew is a really difficult language, because it's a whole other alphabet and you read it the wrong way around, from right to left instead of left to right. Mostly I learned to sound out the words, but I didn't always know their meaning, which kind of bothered me. How could you pray in a language you didn't even understand? Ben-o told me it was like that in his old church, only with Latin, not Hebrew. Then his mom decided that was too old-fashioned, so they started attending a church where they pray in English, which made a lot more sense to me. I wondered why the Jews hadn't thought of the same thing.

Sheila ignored Ryan's question. "I'm surprised you're having one, Tara," she said to me, her eyes lingering on the gold *om* pendant—the one Nanaji gave me for my tenth birthday—that I wore on a fuchsia satin cord around my neck. She wrinkled her nose as if she smelled something unpleasant.

"Why?" I asked.

"Because you're not even Jewish," she said. "Technically."

Not Jewish? That was a new low, even for Sheila Rosenberg. I fixed her with my blankest stare until she got nervous. "You know," she said, twisting a strand of hair around her finger. "Your mother's not Jewish, so you're not Jewish."

"Says who?" I whirled on her.

"Says everyone. You know the saying: 'You are what your mother is.'"

Those sounded like fighting words to me. "What is my mother, exactly?"

Sheila shrugged. "Not a Jew."

That was when I shoved her. You know how parents and teachers are always telling little kids to use their words instead of, like, their fists? Well, I go blank when I'm angry, and I don't have any words. If I did, I would have told Sheila Rosenberg that my mother, who was born in India, converted to Judaism way before I was even born. Not that it was any of her stupid business. So I shoved. And she shoved back, and then we were girl-fighting for real. She got this wild look in her eye, hissing and biting like a trapped cat.

"Girl fight! Girl fight!" Ryan and Adam yelled, pointing at us.

I got Sheila into a modified headlock, mostly to stop her biting.

"Not again, Tara." Rebecca groaned.

That kind of snapped me back to the moment. When Rebecca pulled us apart, I had a hank of Sheila's curly black hair in my fist. I didn't even know how that happened, or when.

Rebecca stood between us, ready to spring into action if either of us made another move, but the moment had passed. Sheila started to cry, her lower lip blubbing in and out like a moist rubber fish. Still, she had been asking for it with that crack about my mother, *and* she was the one doing the biting. And besides, I mean—big deal. She certainly had enough hair. I straightened the hem of my shirt.

"Why'd you stop them? That was awesome," crowed Adam.

Rebecca turned and grabbed him by the collar, lifting him up so he had to stand on his toes to keep his feet on the ground. Rebecca is pretty tough. She's the captain of the basketball team and used to dealing with unruly players.

"You wouldn't want me to tell Rabbi Aron you were involved in a fight, would you?" Rebecca asked him in her most quietly threatening voice, the one she learned from her dad, who's both a union negotiator and a judo master. He never raises his voice, or his hand, but everyone listens to him. "I mean, considering how much trouble you're already in." Adam blinked helplessly. She let him go with a scowl and he slumped against the wall.

Rebecca turned back to me and Sheila. "I don't suppose you're going to apologize to each other?"

Apologize? I opened my mouth to protest, not a hundred percent sure if I could form words yet, but Rebecca shot me a warning look. Sheila looked down and shook her head. Trying not to cry again, I thought.

Rebecca looked at her watch: four thirty. "Time for class. Sheila—you may wanna clean up this situation first," she said, indicating the area around her eyes.

Was that mascara? Sheila sniffled and nodded. She went into the girls' bathroom. Rebecca dragged me toward our classroom, at the far end of the hall.

I grunted, trying to say something, but she shushed me.

"Don't talk," she said.

"I— She—"

"Silence," she said, holding up her hand. "Get all your words back before you start spewing." Rebecca knows me *that* well.

When I had stopped harrumphing, Rebecca used her quiet, scary voice on me. "You can't keep *hitting* people," she said. "You're almost thirteen."

And I thought to myself, *That's a rule? Teenagers don't hit?* How come I didn't know that? Seemed like everyone else knew how to act their age, except me and maybe Ryan Berger. This almost-teenage stuff was bewildering.

"Do you really want to be known as *that* girl?" she asked.

"No, no," I said, still panting. Whatever "that" meant— it sure didn't sound good.

I could see that Rabbi Aron was already inside the classroom, writing something on the board. Which was a lucky break—he hadn't seen us fighting. I mean, I'd never heard of anyone getting expelled from Hebrew school, but I liked Rabbi Aron and I wanted him to like me, and suddenly I felt kind of ashamed—not because of Sheila, but because I had lost control, like a little kid.

A few minutes later, Sheila slipped into a seat in the front row, looking fresh and composed, as if nothing had happened. I don't know how some girls do that. I mean— once I'm on, I'm *on*.

With my adrenaline still pumping, I couldn't concentrate much in class, even though Rabbi Aron is one of my all-time favorite teachers, after Mr. H. Now that I had my words back, I thought of like a hundred different ways I could have replied to Sheila, none of them polite. But I couldn't stop thinking about what she had said. And even though I knew she was a total ignoramus, it made me wonder: Why *was* I doing this? No one in my family is particularly religious, except maybe for Gran. She's active in her synagogue, but whether it's from feeling or habit, it's hard to tell. Mum surprised everyone, including Daddy, when she decided to convert to Judaism before their wedding. But even she only admires the religion from a respectful distance. Daddy hasn't been inside a synagogue since his own bar mitzvah, twelve hundred years ago. Well—except for their wedding, I guess.

Mum's the one who thought I needed to get in touch with my Jewish self, which is a laugh. Believe me, I am *way* in touch with my Jewish side, thanks to Gran. I wouldn't mind getting more in touch with my Indian side, which, if you ask me, is more interesting, and I prefer the cuisine. Mum says I don't have "sides," that ethnicity is not the same as religion, and that anyway, you can't be half-Jewish. Just regular Jewish. And since she is, that's what I am, too.

So maybe having a bat mitzvah wasn't my idea originally, and maybe I hadn't completely made up my own mind about it, but who was that know-it-all Sheila Rosenberg, with her big hair and rubbery lips and runny mascara, to wrinkle her nose at my *om* necklace and say whether I'm Jewish enough to have one or not? I stared at the back of her smug, composed, curly-haired head and made up my mind:

I am having a bat mitzvah, Sheila, I thought at her, *and you're not invited.*

I opened my new datebook and flipped to the page in December corresponding to the Saturday before Hanukkah. My bat mitzvah date. I circled it.

I couldn't wait to tell Mum I was going through with it.

Chapter 4

ll the way home, I imagined how pleased Mum was going to be with my decision. I wasn't going to tell her any of what Sheila had said about me not being Jewish, because I knew it would push her buttons. And if she found out we were fighting—like, physically fighting— that would be a whole new level of trouble. I was just going to deliver the good news.

When I got home, I hurried to her office, stopping only to drop my books on the kitchen table.

"Uh-uh-uh," Daddy said. "Dinner's almost ready."

"Okay," I said, dropping them on the floor instead.

"Kiss for the chef?" The kitchen smelled delicious, like cumin and cilantro. Daddy was making *aloo gobhi*—potatoes and cauliflower. My favorite side dish. I gave him a hug. "Tell your mother dinner in ten," he said. I gave him a thumbs-up.

"Mum?" I called, knocking on her office door.

"It's open, Tara."

When I looked in, Mum was typing away in the dark. Her hair was tied in a loose bun, and she had on what Daddy calls her "hot librarian" glasses—squarish horn-rims that on anyone else would look nerdy but on my mother just looked expensive and sophisticated. The sun had set while she was concentrating on her work, and she hadn't noticed. I flicked on the overhead light. She looked up and smiled.

"Thanks, baby."

"I've come to a decision," I said solemnly, taking a deep breath. "I'm going to go ahead and have a bat mitzvah." I gave her my megawatt smile and waited for her praise.

Instead, she just took off her reading glasses and looked at me. "Was that ever a question?"

"What do you mean?" I asked, my megawatt smile fading.

"Your father and I booked the hall ages ago."

My megawatt smile disappeared completely. "You did what?"

"My God, Tara, do you know how hard it is to get a reception hall? We've had it booked for two years, ever since you started Hebrew school."

So much for keeping an open mind. Mum's face went pale, as if she were suddenly struck by the possibility that I might have refused to go through with it—or might still. She knew if I dug in my heels, there'd be no going back. I felt my jaw tighten and a lump form in my throat. I tried to keep my cool, not lose my words again. Just for one moment, couldn't I have the illusion of choosing my own destiny?

I'd been so excited to tell her my decision, and now the moment was ruined.

For a second I felt like really refusing, just to get back at her for this and maybe gain some control of my life. But making up my mind to have a bat mitzvah had been a big decision, and even though I'd made it in the heat of the moment, it still felt right. Not just a reaction to stupid Sheila Rosenberg. She didn't deserve that much credit.

"Isn't this what you wanted, Tara? Like all your friends?"

All my friends? I mean, sure, Rebecca's Jewish—*Goldstein*, hello? But Ben-o? Catholic. And that was just my BFFs. My friends were all over the map, ethnically speaking. So who or what was Mum talking about?

"It's what *you've* wanted," I told her.

"I want it for you, yes. Not for myself."

"What if it's not what I want?" I asked, biting my lip.

"You just *said* it is," she said, losing patience. "Besides, it's important to your grandmother."

That part was true. Gran never had a bat mitzvah of her own, because in the old days girls weren't allowed. She never had any daughters, either, only Daddy and Uncle Robert, and Uncle Robert has only boys, too—my cousins Avi and Jonathan. So I'm the only girl.

"Such *naches*—such joy—I should live to see my only granddaughter become a bas mitzvah," Gran once told me. Only Gran still says *bas*, the Yiddish way, when everyone else says *bat*, the proper Hebrew way, now. Well, Gran and Mum, since Mum learned most of what she knows about Judaism from Gran.

"Ooh, that reminds me," Mum said, snapping her fingers and reaching for a pen. She jotted down a note on a sticky pad, tore off the page, and stuck it to her computer monitor. "We need to start shopping."

"What?"

"For dresses."

"Dresses, as in *plural*?" I squeaked. I hadn't worn a dress since I was old enough to start dressing myself when I was like four. Unlike Sheila Rosenberg, who wore purple dresses every day. She was a miniature version of her mother in every way, which is not a great look for a thirteen-year-old.

My mother is extremely fashion conscious. Sometimes I wonder how we ended up together.

"You'll be going to at least half a dozen bar mitzvahs," she pointed out. "You can't wear jeans and sneakers."

I groaned. Shopping with Mum is an all-day event. Multiplied by six dresses—the torture was unimaginable. I tried bargaining.

"One dress," I said. "I'll change up the accessories."

"Don't be ridiculous, Tara. No one wears the same dress six times. People will notice."

"Nahee!" I wailed, putting my hands up to my face in mock-horror, like a Bollywood heroine. Being noticed, especially for being different—that was Mum's fear, not

mine. I dropped my hands. "They'll make fun of me for any dress. It's so not me."

"It's the new you," Mum said firmly. "We're going to Macy's on Saturday—mark your calendar. By next month, we'll be shopping for *your* bat mitzvah dress." She sounded almost blissful about it. I just wanted to scream. I really think she should have been Rebecca's mother instead of mine. They could go shoe shopping together and drink mocha lattes.

Mum looked at the clock. "Tara, sweetie, I'm sorry, I need to finish this proposal before supper. Can we continue this talk later?"

"Fine." I sighed, defeated, knowing we probably wouldn't. Mum is a champion conflict avoider. We heard the sound of pots and pans banging around in the kitchen. "Oh, right," I said. "Daddy said to tell you dinner's ready, like, now."

"Who's hungry?" Daddy called, as if on cue.

"Me!" I yelled back.

"Tell your father I need ten more minutes—five," said Mum. "Be good and set the table for him."

"Like I have a choice?" I asked spitefully, closing the door as I left.

I dragged my feet as I walked back to the kitchen, hoping the table would have magically set itself by the time I got there. No such luck.

"Perfect timing," Daddy said, handing me three sets of silverware. He stopped when he saw my expression. "Why the long face?"

I shrugged.

"Out with it," he insisted.

"Nothing . . . It's just . . . I thought having a bat mitzvah or not was supposed to be *my* decision."

"It is your decision. You made up your mind a long time ago."

"I did not! I agreed to go to Hebrew school and *see*." My tears welled up and I stamped my foot in frustration. I was *not* going to cry. I was *not*.

Daddy scratched his head. "I don't remember it that way, sweetie."

Figures, I thought, sulking. Daddy only remembered what he wanted to remember. I grabbed dinner plates out of the dishwasher. "These are clean, right?"

"I'm not sure. Mum is on dish duty this week. Take the ones from the cupboard."

I stomped over to the pantry and flung the door wide.

"Tara—"

"What?" I spat.

"If you want to discuss this, we can do it civilly, over dinner."

"Discuss what?" Mum asked, sliding into her seat. Her attention was already elsewhere, which filled me with outrage.

"Mum!" I wailed.

"Oh, Tara, we're not still talking about this, are we?"

"You said we could continue this discussion."

"There's nothing to discuss," she said, snapping open a

napkin and spreading it across her lap decisively. "You said you made up your mind to go through with it. Your father and I couldn't be more pleased. Now please pass the *aloo gobhi*."

"It's the principle of the thing," I muttered.

We ate in cold silence for a few minutes. I could hear all three of us chewing. I saw a sympathetic look pass between Mum and Daddy, but no one spoke.

"You know what's going to be fun?" Mum said after a while. "Choosing the menu and the decorations and your cake. Wouldn't you like that?"

I scowled. I knew what she was trying to do—trick me into feeling better just because I got to decide on the food. I wasn't falling for it. I had wanted to decide whether to *have* a bat mitzvah, not what to serve once people got there. *Nice try, Mum,* I thought.

I took another forkful of potatoes and cauliflower right from the serving bowl. Then I thought of something—a test of how much control I really had, and exactly how far Mum would let me go with this. A chance to personalize the event, see if I could maybe make it a little bit Indian. Like me.

"I can have anything I want?" I asked, trying to sound offhand about it.

"Such as?" Mum asked warily.

"Like, Indian food. Maybe not for the main course—but the appetizers. Like, potato samosas and stuff."

Mum considered, then swallowed. I knew she wasn't thrilled with the idea, but she tried to smile. She owed me that much. It's not that she doesn't like Indian food, of course; she just likes things to be orderly. Separate. "There's a time and a place for everything"—that's one of her favorite sayings.

"I don't see why not," she said gamely.

"I know they do mini *knishes*," Daddy said. "Remember Joanie and Todd's wedding? If they can do *knishes*, I'm pretty sure they can do samosas."

"And *bhel puri*," I added. Mum looked like she was going to choke on her cauliflower.

"Anything you want," said Daddy.

"And *golgappas*."

"Within *reason*," he said. "I don't think the caterer can pull off *golgappas*." He was probably right about that. At least he was paying attention.

"Okay," I said. "I'll come up with something else, then."

I was still angry, but I was calmer now. At least there was some discussion. Not about the thing that mattered, but it was a start. A small one, but a start.

All at once I was exhausted—the fight with Sheila earlier had already kind of wiped me out. I ate a last bite of potatoes and pushed back my chair.

"May I be excused? I have homework to finish." That wasn't true. It was only the second day of school, so homework was still pretty light. I'd finished mine in study hall. I just wanted to go to bed early, put this day behind me, and wake up to a better one tomorrow. Keep up the fight, just not now.

Later, as I drifted off to sleep, I entertained myself imagining what kind of food Sheila Rosenberg would have at her bat mitzvah, given the choice. All purple things, I'd guess . . . eggplant, purple potatoes, red cabbage (which everyone knows is really purple), red onions (ditto), plums, grape Jell-O . . .

That night I dreamed I was drowning in a sea of purple jelly beans.

Chapter 5

he next morning, I waited in the lobby for Ben-o to come down for school.

"Want me to buzz him—your boyfriend?" asked Sal.

"No, thank you," I said curtly. "And he's not my boyfriend." I rolled my eyes as Sal snickered. Was everyone in my business now?

Luckily I heard the sound of Ben-o's door slamming and then his feet shuffling down the stairs. His family lives on the first floor, which for some reason is on the second floor. Ben-o's dad is the building manager. The last manager didn't have any kids, or a wife, so their apartment is really small for four people—Ben-o, his mom and dad, and now the baby, Nina. The board had been trying for years to upgrade them to a bigger apartment, like old Mrs. Donovan's, next door to me. Our rooms would be literally next to each other. When we were like six, we used to fantasize about his family living there and getting our parents to combine our two apartments into one big one. At the time, we couldn't understand why they were against it. Mrs. D really belonged in an old people's home by now, but she'll never move, because her apartment is rent-controlled.

Ben-o skipped the last four steps, sliding down the railing instead. He had his skateboard tucked under his arm.

"I asked you not to do that, young man," Sal scolded him, even though his eyes were still smiling.

"You asked me not to do it *skating*," Ben-o reminded him. "This time I used my butt."

Sal shook his head. He held the door wide and escorted us through with a flourish. *"Mademoiselle, Monsieur, après vous."*

"Merci, Monsieur Sal!" Ben-o said with an exaggerated bow. I rolled my eyes again. One year of middle school French and he thought he was the king of France.

"De rien," said Sal. *"À tout à l'heure, Mademoiselle Tara."*

"I take Spanish," I said.

When we got outside, I asked Ben-o, "Why do you have your board today? Don't tell me you forgot." Meaning: It was Wednesday. And Wednesday, after school, was Robotics Club.

"I didn't forget," Ben-o said, taking off with a running start. After a minute he came back, gliding to a stop next to me. "Listen, do you mind catching up later? I want to try a couple of moves before school."

Since the weekend, he'd been acting so weird and—*unfriendly.* Except for giving me the datebook on Monday, which was weird in itself. I felt the way I sometimes feel after a fight with Rebecca. Only that had never happened with Ben-o before. And I had no idea what I had done or when.

"Whatever," I said.

"Cool," said Ben-o, missing the sarcasm. "See you in science."

"See you in science," I told his backside.

✳ ✳ ✳

"Show of hands, who's coming to Robotics Club this afternoon?" Mr. H asked in science class, the period before lunch. Ben-o and I raised our hands, and so did Ryan Berger and Adam Greenspan. *What?* I tried to catch Ben-o's eye, but he was busy glowering at Ryan Berger.

It turned out Ryan and Adam each had to pick an academic club to avoid suspension for what had happened on the first day of school, and they both picked Robotics. How was that allowed? It seemed like Ryan was suddenly everywhere I turned.

"I can't believe it," I kept saying to Ben-o at lunchtime.

"I can," he replied.

"What do you mean?"

"You. Berger. Do the math."

"Eww!" I said, faking an arm punch. "Gross."

Rebecca had her nose in her math notebook, looking up once in a while to compare notes with Sheila Rosenberg. She happened to look up when I was fake-punching Ben-o, and she looked ready to spring into action again.

"Take it easy, Rebecca!" I said. "I'm not *hitting* anyone."

She pursed her lips and reburied her head in her notebook while simultaneously shoveling down a big pile of tofu scramble. She's terrified of failing math.

"Berger definitely has a thing for you," Ben-o continued.

"Shut up," I said. "He does not."

"According to Adam he does." He shrugged and took an enormous bite of his sandwich.

If Ryan Berger had a "thing" for me, he had a funny way of showing it. Not that the thought had ever crossed my mind.

"At least we're partners," I said aloud.

"Hmm?" said Ben-o.

"Oh—for Robotics, I mean. You and me."

Ben-o nodded and gave a thumbs-up. His mouth was still full of sandwich—ham and provolone. Same as every Wednesday.

"We have a pretty good chance of getting to the finals this year. Not that we have too much competition," I said, glaring at the back of Ryan Berger's head.

Ben-o swallowed and scowled. "Stop obsessing over Berger."

"I'm *not* obsessing. And you're wrong. He's not into me. Not like it would even matter if he was. I'm not into *him*."

"Mmm-hmm," said Ben-o.

If anyone was obsessing, it was Ben-o.

✳ ✳ ✳

After school, at the club meeting, Mr. H was bouncing on his heels. He couldn't wait to tell us about this year's project.

Ben-o and I grabbed our worktable from last year, the one by the window, before anyone else could get it. There were twelve members this year—three more than last year. There were six old-timers, including me and Ben-o. Then there was Ryan and Adam, of course, and a crop of new sixth-graders.

"Ladies and gents," said Mr. H, snapping up the projector screen to reveal the secret written on the board, "start your engines!"

We old-timers let out a cheer. On the board were the two words we'd all been hoping for: RACE CARS!

"And where there are race cars, there's an . . . ?"

"OBSTACLE COURSE," we all yelled.

Ben-o and I did a high-five. Instantly, we put our heads together and started whispering excitedly.

Mr. H cleared his throat. "Before we begin," he said, "Feinstein, O'Connell, may I have a word with you outside?" He called all his favorites by our last names. I assumed he wanted to give us a pep talk, some words of wisdom about the district finals. We followed him into the hallway.

"I'm afraid I have some news for the two of you," he said once the door closed. I smiled, not imagining what he was going to say next. "I'd like you two to split up this year."

"What?" I cried.

"You two are my best. It would be unfair to team you up against the other kids. I thought you could each mentor a new club member."

"Like who?" said Ben-o warily.

"Feinstein, I thought you could work with Ryan," Mr. H said, turning to me.

"Seriously?"

"I'm afraid so, Feinstein."

"He doesn't know the first thing about robots," I complained.

"Precisely where you come in. O'Connell, likewise, I want you to work with Adam."

Talk about unfair advantages. Adam's actually got half a brain, whereas Ryan Berger is a total zero.

I could tell Ben-o didn't like it any better than I did, but he didn't say anything to Mr. H. He just shrugged. When we went back into the lab, he started gathering up his stuff from our worktable.

"Where are you going?" I asked. "This table's big enough for four." I really didn't want to be stranded with Ryan Berger.

"You and your new partner can have this table," he said. "Adam and I will be over there." He caught Adam's eye and chin-pointed to the table in the opposite corner. Adam nodded and walked over.

"Don't be mad," I said. "This isn't my fault."

Ben-o shrugged and slouched away.

"Berger, over here, please," said Mr. H, thumping his hand on my table.

Mr. H distributed a couple of handouts and gave a quick overview of the robotic parts available for our use. I tuned out when he started going over the sign-out process for borrowing electronic equipment, which I knew already.

I'd had a basic concept in mind, since watching the eighth-grade regionals last year, of what I would build if we ever got this project. But it was going to be hard without Ben-o. His design skills were the best, while I was better at actually building things. We needed each other.

Like the robot arm we made for our sixth-grade science fair—it was his idea, mainly. But it was my idea to modify his mom's Roomba vacuum cleaner instead of starting from scratch like he wanted to. That was the only reason we got it done in time. We're a great team like that.

We'd really wanted to get the RoboChat app—which lets you control the Roomba with text messages—and hack in some homegrown voice activation using open-source speech recognition. Only we didn't have enough money for the wireless device it needed, so we scrapped that idea and made our own remote control, which was just okay. We rigged the arm using Ben-o's Erector Set, a bike chain, a sponge gripper, and a couple of micro servomotors we lifted from Mr. H's supply cabinet. It was kind of like the carnival game where you try to win a prize by lowering a motorized claw into a pile of cheap stuffed animals—only, those claws are designed to fail, while ours actually sort of worked. It could pick up objects of different sizes and weights without dropping or crushing them . . . most of the time. It worked great with an empty soda can, a tennis ball, and assorted stuffed animals. Really small things like pencils didn't work. Or heavy things, like a two-liter bottle of soda. We had to adjust the tension like six times before it could pick up a balloon without popping it. There was also a mishap with a full jar of spaghetti sauce, but we didn't mention that in our data.

We won second place in the whole science fair, ahead of the seventh- and eighth-graders. The perfect team. Which was why I had been counting on us being partners again.

✳ ✳ ✳

Totally ignoring Ryan, I walked to the supply cabinet and grabbed two large sheets of graph paper and a mechanical pencil. When I got back to our table, I stared at the blank paper for a long moment, then closed my eyes and breathed in, summoning what little drawing talent I had. That was another thing Ben-o was really great at. Me? Not so much.

While I worked on my sketch, using more eraser than pencil, Ryan entertained himself by doing this stiff-jointed walk and saying "Take me to your leader," as if he thought robots were some kind of zombie alien predators. I imagined how disappointed he was going to be when he figured out this was a *science* club, and not even one where he got to blow things up.

He was being totally annoying, but he knew better than to do anything that might actually get him kicked out of the club or he would be suspended for real, maybe even expelled. *Now, there's an idea*, I thought.

After a while, he dropped the zombie routine and wandered over. "Whatcha doing?"

I crumpled up the paper and threw it away in frustration.

"Come on," he said. He retrieved the paper from the floor and smoothed it out on our worktable. "Show me."

"Okay." I sighed. "I saw this cool thing at regionals last year, but I don't know how to draw it."

Ryan took up the pencil. "I'm listening."

"Well," I said, "it should be low to the ground, like a Lamborghini, but narrower, and with really big wheels in the back. Also kind of pointy in the front, like an airplane."

Ryan drew a pretty decent race car, except he added a sort of tail-fin-looking thing. I almost felt bad telling him that wasn't going to work.

"Like this?" he said.

"Even bigger wheels. But here's the thing—there are definitely going to be some deep curves on the obstacle course, so I want to put in a split torso—approximately here."

"A what?"

"That way, even if the back end flips over a hundred eighty degrees, it'll still land on its wheels and keep driving. But that means no tail fin, okay? No offense."

It didn't matter, though, because Ryan had already reached the limits of his technical comprehension, as well as his attention span. He tossed the pencil in the air a few times and didn't even bother to pick it up off the floor when it fell. He pushed the paper away to rest his head on the table.

I picked up the pencil and got back to work on the drawing, erasing the tail fin and enlarging the wheels. Then Ryan seemed to think of something. He sat up and pulled the drawing back toward him, making me draw a jagged line across the page.

"Hey, look what you did!"

He knit his eyebrows together and scratched his head. "Umm . . . I have a question."

"What?"

"Where's the robot?"

"You're kidding, right?" He wasn't kidding. "The car is the robot." I wanted to add, *Duh*, but instead I said, *"Obviously."*

Ryan bit his lip in concentration. "Wait, then—who's driving?"

"Never mind," I said. "Go back to robot-walking." That would at least get him out of my hair.

I really wanted to brainstorm with Ben-o. When I looked over at their table, he and Adam were already building something out of cardboard. I grabbed the smudged and wrinkled drawing and wandered over.

"What are you guys doing?" I asked, standing on tiptoe to see over the top.

"Securing the perimeter—" said Adam.

"Building a wall," said Ben-o, sounding almost apologetic.

Was he really saying . . . ?

"—so no one can spy on us," Adam finished.

I stared at Ben-o as the insult began to sink in.

"You think I'd copy you guys?" I sputtered. "Please!" I mean, I'd never had to compete against Ben-o before, and I really didn't want to go up against him in the finals, but this was insane. Assuming both our teams made it that far—a big *if*, with Ryan dragging me down.

For a brief moment, I thought about quitting. But I'd been looking forward to Robotics all summer, and I wasn't going to let anyone mess it up for me. Not Ryan, not Adam, not even Ben-o.

"I already have my design figured out," I lied, waving the crumpled paper. "Bet you don't."

"Want me to look at it?" asked Ben-o hopefully. Adam winked and nudged him, as if they were putting one over on me. Ben-o looked uncomfortable.

"No," I said. "Forget it. Wouldn't want to give away any trade secrets."

I clomped back to my table, where Ryan was swinging a rotary belt at a row of nine-volt batteries. I glanced around the room. Ben-o and Adam were busy with duct tape and cardboard. Joe was showing a sixth-grader the supply closet. At the table next to mine, Deshaun and Marina were absorbed in a heated discussion about torque conversion. Trying to imagine me and Ryan having that same conversation made me snort-laugh.

"What?" said Ryan.

"Nothing," I said, shaking my head. "Look, no offense, Ryan, but—why didn't you just join the drama club or something?"

"I dunno," he said, scratching his head. "This sounded more interesting."

"Time," Mr. H called out. "Everyone please start packing up. If you're going to sign something out, do it now. Or put it back where you found it, please."

Ryan whooped and headed for the door.

"Hey! Aren't you forgetting something?" I yelled after him. Ryan stopped and turned around, clearly bewildered. "Um, the batteries? The rotary belt? Could you put them back?"

He just laughed and kept going. *What a jerk!* I gathered up his mess and put everything back in the closet.

"How'd it go today?" Mr. H asked.

"It was fine," I lied. I didn't have the energy to complain about Ryan Berger. I could see him out in the hallway with Ben-o and Adam. I brushed past all of them without stopping. I was going to walk home by myself, to teach Ben-o a lesson. I was halfway down the block when I heard him calling my name.

"Tara, wait up!"

I stopped, but I didn't turn around. Ben-o pulled up next to me on his skateboard.

"The wall was Adam's idea," he said breathlessly. "I just thought it was funny. I didn't mean to hurt your feelings."

"You didn't."

"How was working with Berger?" He snickered.

"Now who's obsessing?" I demanded crossly.

Ben-o stiffened. "Just asking."

"Turns out, Ryan's really great at drawing—almost as

good as you," I said. "I think we're gonna make it to the finals, no problem."

Ben-o's face clouded, but then he tried to make light of it. "That's lucky," he joked. "You can't draw to save your life." Which was a little too true to be funny.

"I have to go," I said. "Study date at Rebecca's."

Ben-o perked up. "For Social Studies? Mind if I join you? I didn't understand that Middle East geography thing at all."

"No, er—Honors English. I heard there's going to be a pop quiz tomorrow."

It was stupid to lie, but I just wanted to get away from him for a while, to punish him for whatever it was he was mad at me for. Which meant I had to walk the long way home; otherwise, he would know I was lying. I cursed myself silently as I left him at Eighty-Seventh Street and pretended to walk to Rebecca's. I just wanted to go home.

Chapter 6

"ise and shine!" Mum sang, snapping open the window shades in my room on Saturday morning.

"What time is it?" I asked groggily.

"Nearly nine thirty."

I groaned. Nine thirty on a Saturday morning? I jammed the pillow over my head to block out the light.

"No, no, no," Mum said, snatching it away. "I told you. We are going dress shopping today. So put your happy game face on, as you kids say."

I've never heard anyone say that.

"Like this?" I grinned and crossed my eyes.

"If that's your happy game face, then yes. Now get dressed."

I put on my typical weekend wear—purposely ripped black jeans held together with safety pins, black hoodie, neon pink socks. Ninja style. With a splash of color.

Over breakfast, she kept trying, and failing, to put a good spin on it. "Nothing too, too fancy. Something chic and fun. Something 'kicky.'"

"Mum—*kicky*? I don't even know what that means."

"We'll save the fancy dress for your own bas mitzvah," she added, ignoring me. "Hopefully you'll have grown a bit by then."

I peered down my own shirt. "Nope."

"Don't be vulgar, Tara. And go put on a training bra."

"For *what*?"

"You need to wear it to see how it fits under a dress."

I buried my head in my hands. Pointless. "I don't know where I put it," I lied.

"It's in your top drawer. No doubt with the tags still attached. Go."

I stalked back to my room and fished the itchy, icky thing out of my dresser drawer. *Why, why, why?* It fit like an infant bikini top—completely pointless. I wriggled it on over my head and put my sweatshirt back on. It made no difference whatsoever.

"Where are you two ladies off to?" Daddy asked as we were leaving.

"Macy's," said Mum.

"My condolences," he said.

"Thank you," Mum and I both answered.

Mum was in a terrible mood from the start. She began criticizing my posture on the subway and even yelled at me at Macy's for riding the escalator backward, which I always do. And the dresses—*ugh*.

"How about *this*?" she asked, pulling out a long-sleeved velvet number that was almost as tall as she was.

"Too long."

"This one's cute," she said, trying again with a blue satin minidress.

"Too short."

If she wouldn't let me wear my normal clothes, then I'd rather do something vintage, maybe repurpose an old dress of hers or even Gran's. Or one of Daddy's old suits cut down for me. That would be cool. Mum would probably die of embarrassment. Which would be part of the fun.

Mum could be so uptight about stuff like that. I guess in high school, when she lived with Meena Auntie, she only got to wear hand-me-downs because Meena couldn't afford to buy her sister new clothes. That meant wearing Meena's old-ladyish *salwar kameezes* instead of the designer jeans and sweatshirts everybody else was wearing.

I wasn't clear on all the details, because Mum never liked talking about it. Meena Auntie was in law school at the time and became Mum's legal guardian so she could bring her to the U.S. for high school. Mum never got over being the outsider, mocked for her clothes, her accent, and the strong-smelling curries Meena made her carry to school every day in a round steel tiffin box. One time, it leaked all over her school bag and her clothes and looked, Mum said, like diarrhea. I mean, I love Indian food, but I can't imagine carrying it to school and having to eat it cold from a leaky, three-tiered tiffin. Mum was happier before she came to the U.S., but the catch is, now she couldn't stand to live anywhere else. And somehow that was Meena's fault, too. I guess that's just something that happens between siblings. Not that I would *know*. But it did explain why the idea of vintage really freaked her out. *Used clothing—on purpose? The horror!*

"Stop scratching your chest, Tara. Here, you can't object to this one," she said, holding up a knee-length dress with purple and white stripes.

"Too Sheila Rosenberg," I said.

Mum sighed. She can be fairly clueless sometimes. First of all, we wasted like an hour in the wrong department. Anything designed to be held up with a pair of boobs is obviously not going to work for me, training bra or no. And the girls' department was even worse. I mean—*really, Mum? Pink chiffon?* Not with my complexion.

After two hours of bickering and no dresses, Mum heaved herself into a tall seat at the makeup counter, thrusting her jacket and purse at me. "Shanette, dear," she said, reading the woman's name tag, "I need a fresh-up."

As Shanette prepared to apply new makeup over Mum's old makeup, I played with the lipsticks and eyeliners on the counter, twisting them up and down, smelling them, trying to imagine why anyone would leave home with this sticky stuff on her face. I really didn't get the attraction, even though lots of girls in my grade had started wearing eyeliner. I couldn't even draw a straight line. Not that that stopped some people. Sometimes Rebecca and I gave each other crazy makeovers, but only in my room. I wondered if Mum was going to try to make me wear makeup for my bat mitzvah. Probably. I made a mental note not to wear mascara, after what had happened to Sheila Rosenberg. Not that I was planning to cry. But it might rain or something—better to be safe.

I've noticed that Mum will only stop for a "fresh-up" if there's a woman of color at the counter, because white women don't understand her skin—they'll slather on a foundation color that's either too light, making her look like a circus clown, or too dark, so she looks like she's wearing a mask. I couldn't blame anyone for being confused—on the counter was a massive color wheel with about a thousand different skin tones multiplied by four different "undertones"—apparently you were supposed to know both to find your perfect shade. I gave the outer wheel a spin, and it randomly landed on ebony.

"Stop playing with that, Tara."

"Mum, am I a Warm or a Cool?"

"A what?"

"Do I have pinkish, yellowish, olive, or brown undertones?"

"You don't need foundation, Tara."

"I know. I'm just asking."

Shanette lifted my chin, tilting my head this way and that. "I would say your tone is a light brownish," she said. "Wheat, to be precise. With a touch of honey."

Personally, I would have said oatmeal, with grayish-blah undertones, but honey wheat sounded nice. Like something delicious. I turned back to the color wheel, lining up the two parts. Honey plus Wheat—that made me a Warm. *Look for yellow, gold, or peach-based makeup shades.* Okay! I grabbed a Coral Lush lip pencil from the counter display and carefully drew a large pink *bindi* dot between my eyebrows. I bunched up my lips like Aishwarya Rai, the Indian movie star, and gave myself a long, sexy look in the magnifying mirror, drawing Mum's scratchy linen scarf across my face like a silk *dupatta*. That was when it hit me.

"Mummy," I said, "I have an excellent idea."

"Yes, love?" she murmured, through slightly parted lips as Shanette applied powder all over her face with a large, soft brush.

"For *my* bat mitzvah, I think I'll wear Meena Auntie's sari."

I thought Mum would like that. It wasn't like wearing a hand-me-down. It was something more special than that—an heirloom. She couldn't possibly object. The sari was very expensive and old, with lots of family history. It had once belonged to my great-grandmother, who had passed it on to Meena Auntie, who passed it on to me because she doesn't have a daughter, only Vijay. It seemed to me the kind of "lovely gesture" that Mum was always talking about. Plus, it wasn't technically a dress. Bonus. I turned and smiled, anticipating Mum's pleasure.

"Tara," Mum said through her teeth while Shanette painted a wide, Heavenly Hibiscus gash across her mouth. "There is a time and a place for everything."

I was surprised by her reaction—hurt, too. This wasn't

the same as having potato samosas—this was different. Special. A way to have a little piece of Nanaji there with me. In other words—I wasn't kidding.

"You will do no such thing," she continued. "You will not be having some . . . some—*basmati bas mitzvah!*"

I had a good laugh at that, actually. When Mum gets flustered, she sounds exactly like her mother—my *nani*—making up silly bilingual puns and alliterations on the fly. It's something all Indians do, like the billboard for Amul butter I saw when we visited Mumbai that said, "Let *bhaingans* be byegones!" *Bhaingan* being eggplant. I had no clue why that was supposed to be funny.

I decided to play it straight and have some fun at her expense, to get back at her.

"Good one, Mum, except it's *bat* mitzvah. No one says *bas* nowadays. 'Basmati *bat* mitzvah.' I love it!"

"Seriously, Tara."

"It's a great idea," I said, acting all serious. "We can serve *pullao* on a big star-shaped platter."

"Tara," she said in a warning tone.

"Yes, exactly!" I said. *Tara* means "star" in Hindi, after all. "And instead of throwing candy at the *bimah*, everyone can throw basmati rice, like at a wedding." I smirked.

"Enough, Tara."

"Or they can throw marigolds, like in India. I love marigolds, don't you, Mum? I'd like my corsage to be marigolds." I'd been obsessed with marigolds, and Indian weddings, ever since seeing *Monsoon Wedding* on cable over the summer.

"Tara, you take a thing too, too far," Mum said in the singsongy Indian accent that comes out when I'm aggravating her.

"But you said—"

"I *said* you can have a say in the arrangements. I did not say you could make a mockery of everything."

That was harsh. I had mostly been kidding about the other stuff, but I was way serious about the sari. If I could choose the decorations and the menu and the cake, then why not my outfit, too? If I wanted to *desi* it up—"Indify" it a little, honor Nanaji by wearing my sari—then why not? It was my party.

Besides, it was just *clothes*. Mum, of all people, knew you could express yourself with what you wear. Why couldn't I express my Indian heritage and my Jewish one at the same time?

"You are wiping that—that *shmutz* off your face. Right now."

"Here, try these new makeup-removal towelettes!" Shanette put in, tearing open a little packet for me. I have to admit, it worked really well—took the pink stuff right off and wasn't greasy or anything. I pocketed the rest of the samples for the next time Rebecca came over.

"You should get these, Mum," I said. "So you don't wake up with kohl eyes in the morning."

"Twelve ninety-five for one drop of aloe vera lotion on a paper towel?" Mum said with contempt. "Nothing doing."

Shanette looked disappointed. She went back to applying Mum's fresh-up.

I wanted to go home so badly. I was sick of shopping and annoyed with Mum for being so conventional. This fitting-in business was never for me. It actually made me feel *more* self-conscious, like there was something weird about me that everyone could see except me.

Keeping things orderly and separate may have made Mum feel more in control of her life, but me? It made me feel like someone with multiple personality disorder— make that multiple ethnicity disorder.

I knew where she was coming from, but it had nothing to do with me and what I wanted. Just because *she* hated going to high school in the U.S. didn't mean I was going to. I definitely didn't hate middle school. I kept telling her that things were different now from when she was a kid, but I don't think she got it. I wasn't even the only Asian kid in my Hebrew school. Well, Asian-*looking*—Adam Greenspan was adopted, so it's not as if either of his parents is Asian. And nobody gives him a hard time, not even his best friend, Ryan Berger, who's not exactly the most thoughtful person on the planet.

Anyway, this wasn't the "time" or the "place" for a real argument, so I tried to sit quietly and not pick a fight. But Shanette was taking *forever* with the eye shadow, showing Mum how to "accentuate" the crease in her eyelid. I didn't know that was supposed to be a good thing.

"Sit *still*, Tara," Mum said when I accidentally kicked Shanette, causing her to goof up Mum's left eye.

"Sorry," I said. "Restless leg."

Shanette wiped off the eye shadow and started again. I stifled a groan. I needed to get away from Mum for a few minutes.

"Can I go downstairs and get a shake at the Cellar? Please?"

"You'll ruin your lunch," Mum said.

"But I'm hungry *now*." I put some extra whine into it, knowing it would irritate her into saying yes. "Please?"

Mum sighed. "Take money from my wallet. But I want you back here in five minutes. You hear me, Tara? Five."

"Okay!" I called over my shoulder. I was already past the accessories counter. I headed downstairs to the Cellar via Small Leather Goods. To make myself feel better, I rode the escalator backward.

While I was waiting in line at the ice cream counter, someone tapped me on the shoulder, and I turned around. Of all people, it was Ryan Berger and his permanent sidekick, Adam Greenspan. As if I had conjured them up just by thinking about them five minutes earlier. That was a disturbing thought.

"Oh. My. *Gawd!* Tara Feinstein," Ryan said. He stuck out his hip and pointed at me, imitating some gum-chewing airheads in our grade. "Random!"

"What are you doing here?" I asked, eyeing them both with suspicion.

"Getting ice cream, same as you," Ryan said.

I thought about what Ben-o had said on Wednesday, about Ryan Berger having a "thing" for me, which was totally gross. But it was true that everywhere I went, there he was. Random, my butt.

"At Macy's, I mean. Are you following me?"

"Nice ego," Ryan said, holding up a shopping bag. "Shirt and tie. For my bar mitzvah."

"Without your mom?"

"She's here. Upstairs, I mean. In No-Man's Land."

"Oh." I nodded. "Lingerie." The very thought made me itchy again.

"Yup."

The line started to move forward. "Well, see ya," I said, turning my back to him. A moment later, he tapped my shoulder again. "What do you want, Ryan?"

"Can we cut in? Behind you?"

I couldn't believe the *chutzpah*. Ryan Berger and I may have been partners in Robotics, but that didn't make us friends. Then we "randomly" run into each other at Macy's and he thinks he can chat-cut? No way.

"No way," I said.

"Come on," he insisted. "We'll reverse-cut."

"That's between you and the people behind me," I said. But behind me was a mom with four little kids who were all over the place, and she said she didn't mind if my "little friends" wanted to join me. *Blech.* I kept my back to Ryan and Adam and pretended to be super-interested in the menu painted on the wall above the counter, even though I knew exactly what I was going to have. Vanilla shake, one pump of chocolate syrup. Same as always.

Ryan tapped me a third time, which was starting to get on my nerves. "Can Adam borrow a dollar? He's a little short." He practically fell over, he was laughing so hard at his own joke. Adam stood there grinning like an idiot, not at all insulted by the joke about his height. I wonder why he takes it.

One time in fifth grade, Ryan called me a Hin-Jew, which was totally ignorant, because how would he even know if my Indian family was Hindu or not? There are like a thousand different religions in India, even Judaism. When I told my dad, he just laughed and said that was a good one, but he didn't hear it the way Ryan had said it. Daddy said you have to have a sense of humor about things or you end up holding grudges your whole life, like Gran. *And Mum*, I thought, but he didn't say that.

Anyway, I lent Adam the dollar, but I doubted I'd ever see it again.

"Why do you keep scratching under your arm?" asked Ryan.

I didn't say, "BECAUSE MY STUPID BRA ITCHES!" Instead, I gave him a murderous look, and he backed off. Then it was my turn to order. Ryan and Adam walked up to the counter with me.

"Together or separate?" the ice cream lady asked.

"Separate!" I barked.

Adam was served first, and his ice cream cone was already starting to melt by the time I got my shake.

"You better not drip on my new stuff," said Ryan, shifting the shopping bag away from Adam. "My mom'll have a cow."

"You should see the bow tie his mom made him get." Adam snorted. "It's really dorky."

"No, it's not," said Ryan. "It's cool—for a tie, I mean. Wanna see, Tara?"

"Not particularly," I said, slurping my shake.

Ryan shrugged. "I guess you'll see it at my bar mitzvah, then."

"I will?" That was a surprise. "I didn't think I was invited."

"Of course you are. My mom said I have to invite everyone."

"Gee, thanks."

"I would have invited you anyway," he said. "But not Sheila Rosenberg, probably."

"Please," I said, holding up my hand. "Don't put Sheila Rosenberg and me in the same sentence."

"Just let her tell *me* I'm not Jewish," Adam declared, recalling our fight. "I'll punch her in the nose."

It's interesting, when you think about it. Here was this Korean-born Jewish kid named Adam Greenspan. Yet his best friend—the same jerk who called me a Hin-Jew in fifth grade—didn't even seem to find anything remarkable about him, other than his height. He would never call Adam a name like that, even though Adam probably wouldn't care.

"She's bigger than you," I reminded Adam.

"I can take her."

"Go for the hair," I advised.

Ryan hooted. "See ya tomorrow, T," he said.

"See ya, T," Adam echoed.

"Yeah."

Did Ryan Berger really just invite me to his bar mitzvah? Well, *that* was weird.

Chapter 7

Gran was there when we came home from Macy's, empty-handed. She had let herself in while we were out. Walking is her favorite exercise, and she only lives about fifteen blocks away, so she almost always makes a "pit stop" at our place.

She was sitting at the kitchen table playing solitaire. Mum's lip curled in irritation.

"Ruthie," she said, smiling tightly. "Make yourself at home."

"Don't mind if I do," said Gran evenly, shuffling the deck.

"Is Joshua home?"

"Haven't seen him," said Gran. "I used my own key."

"Of course you did," Mum muttered, sucking her teeth.

Mum and Gran don't have the warmest relationship. A really long time ago, before Mum and Daddy were even married, Mum called Gran a *yenta*—a busybody—right to her face. She wasn't trying to insult her—she didn't even know what it meant. She had heard Daddy call Gran that behind her back and thought it was Gran's nickname or some kind of term of endearment, like *bubeleh* or something. Gran never forgave her for it, even though Daddy's the one she should have been mad at.

Gran had really wanted Daddy to marry a "nice Jewish girl." Mum's converting to Judaism should have made her happy, but, truthfully, nothing Mum does makes Gran happy. Gran is a champion grudge holder. It's one of the few things they have in common.

Mum shut herself in her office. I went into my room and brought out the sari to show Gran, getting it out of the special cedar box Meena Auntie had given me for safekeeping.

The sari was dark pink, black, white, and a deep red Mum called crimson. It also had real gold embroidery and a lime green border—a combination you'd never think of, but it worked somehow. Mum said it was too sophisticated for me at my age, but I thought it was the most beautiful thing in the world.

Sometimes Rebecca and I would take it out of the box and put on an old Indian CD and spin around and around in it, like a starlet in some Bollywood dance number. I always folded it back carefully when we were done, though. I knew how to take care of nice things.

"Fancy-schmancy," Gran said, pushing out her lower lip and nodding her approval. Gran loves anything with a lot of bling to it. "And look at those colors—can you believe it? Leave it to the *goyim* to come up with something like that.

Is that what your mother's wearing to your bas mitzvah?"

"Why does everyone *assume* I'm having one?"

"A what—a bas mitzvah? What are you talking about? Of course you're having one."

"Says who?"

"Says me. It takes a *simcha*—a happy event—to bring the whole family together. How else can I get my *no-goodnik* older son and that wife of his to visit me?"

In point of fact, Gran didn't care that much about Uncle Robert and Aunt Charlotte, but she misses her grandsons, my cousins Avi and Jonathan. They live in Cincinnati. We don't see them very often, mostly because Aunt Charlotte is terrified of New York City.

Anyway, she was right—they'd definitely come to my bat mitzvah, even though Charlotte recently told Gran she was surprised Mum and Daddy were raising me in the "Jewish tradition." Whatever that meant.

"What tradition should they raise her in? Buddhism?" Gran had snapped.

"Oh, is that what Rita practices?" Charlotte reportedly asked. Gran wouldn't tell me how she answered that, except to tell me that Charlotte's got a screw loose.

"Why is being Buddhist any screwier than being Jewish?" I asked her.

"Don't talk crazy," Gran said. "And don't tell your mother, okay? I got enough *tsuris*—aggravation."

"Why don't *you* have a bat mitzvah, Gran?" I asked her now.

"Me? Don't talk crazy. Who wants to see an *alter kocker* make a fool of herself?"

"I might enjoy that," I teased. *Alter kocker* means, basically, "old fart."

Gran shook her fist at me. "You're a lousy kid, you know that?"

"So I've been told." I started to fold the sari and put it back in its cedar box.

"Since when does your mother wear a sari anymore?"

"Not Mum," I said. "I was thinking *I'd* wear it, Gran."

"You?" Gran said. "You're flat as a matzoh. You couldn't hold it up with suspenders."

"Look who's talking," I retorted, stopping to rest my elbow on her puffy white hair. Gran is about four feet tall with her Shabbos shoes on, and bent over like a question mark. Which is totally appropriate, because she's the most inquisitive person I know.

"Fresh! We're not talking about me. Get off. I just had my hair done."

"When?" I asked, feigning innocence.

"Two days ago!"

"Two *days!*" I teased. "You haven't washed your hair in *two days*?"

"I get my hair done once a week, and you know it," she said, fluffing up the spot where my elbow had penetrated the crunchy helmet of hair spray. "What are you *kratsn*—scratching at?"

"Mum made me wear a training bra. It itches."

"*Feh!*" said Gran. "A waste of material."

She was right about that, too. It was weird going back to school and seeing which girls had suddenly sprouted boobs over the summer—not that I was going around staring at people's chests; it was just hard not to notice. In the yes column: Sheila Rosenberg, Jenna Alberts, Missy Abrams. In the no column: me, Rebecca, Aisha Khan. I wouldn't even care if it weren't for all this drama about my bat mitzvah dress. Mum is a normal, average size—a lot smaller than Meena Auntie, a whole lot bigger than Gran—so I suppose I had nothing to worry about in the long run. It just made me wonder if I was going to wake up one morning soon in a totally different body. I kept checking, but so far, I was still me. Yet another good reason to go for a sari, I thought—you couldn't outgrow one.

I was regaling Gran with horror stories about the selection at Macy's when Mum came back into the kitchen to pour herself a glass of water. I could tell she had switched gears and was now thinking about one of her building plans, because her eyes seemed to be focused on something invisible about a foot in front of her face.

"Macy's—*feh!*" Gran was saying. "You'll go see my nephew Marvin."

Mum rolled her eyes.

"What?" said Gran. "You think the *goyim*—pardon me, the non-Jews—don't shop on the Lower East Side, I got news for you."

Of course Mum knows the meaning of *goyim*. Along with *shiksa*—a not-nice word for a girl who isn't Jewish. It's one of Gran's most frequent Yiddish vocabulary words.

"Tomorrow we're going to Bloomingdale's," Mum said. I moaned.

"Why don't you let her wear the sari like she wants?" Gran said. "It'll be a real standout."

Mum gave Gran a pointed look, but Gran waved her hand dismissively. "Eh, that was entirely different," she said.

"What are you guys talking about?"

"Ask your mother," Gran said.

"You mean Mum's wedding dress?"

"Enough, Tara," Mum said.

Famously, Mum had worn a traditional red bridal sari to her own wedding, under pressure from Nani, who wept when she found out Mum was planning to wear a white gown. "Like a widow," Nani had cried, wringing her hands. Mum was mortified, but she finally caved and wore the bright red-and-gold sari, which thoroughly scandalized Daddy's Jewish relatives, especially Gran, who said only a *nafka*—a really, really mean word I refuse to translate— wore red to her own wedding. Mum had regretted the decision ever since, even though I've seen the pictures and she looked absolutely gorgeous. I hope to look even a little bit like her when I grow up.

In other words, "standing out" was the last thing Mum wanted. With her chestnut brown hair and dark eyes, some people at our synagogue mistook her for a Sephardic Jew, from Israel or Spain. She never corrected them, even though she spoke no Hebrew, or Spanish.

"Bloomingdale's," she repeated emphatically.

"But I have Hebrew school tomorrow."

"After that."

"But Rebecca's coming for lunch."

"Before that. It doesn't have to take a lot of time, if you stay focused."

We heard a key in the lock. "Anybody home?" Daddy yelled.

"In here!" I yelled back. Daddy came into the kitchen with two cloth grocery sacks from the farmers' market.

"Bloomingdale's?" Gran shrugged, turning back to Mum. "Suit yourself."

"What's going on?" said Daddy.

"We have to go shopping again, for dumb dresses."

"Just maybe," he said, putting down the grocery bags, "you ought to be less concerned with what you're going to wear and focus more on the sanctity of the occasion."

Well, that was kind of my point, wasn't it? I wished I had expressed it like that myself. More than anything, I hated being misunderstood.

"Maybe if I didn't have to go dress shopping, I could spend more time studying my haftarah," I pointed out.

"Well played," Daddy admitted. "What do you say, Rita?"

"Bloomingdale's. Tomorrow. End of story."

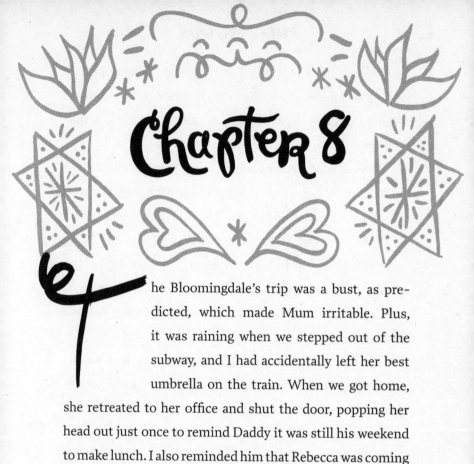

Chapter 8

he Bloomingdale's trip was a bust, as predicted, which made Mum irritable. Plus, it was raining when we stepped out of the subway, and I had accidentally left her best umbrella on the train. When we got home, she retreated to her office and shut the door, popping her head out just once to remind Daddy it was still his weekend to make lunch. I also reminded him that Rebecca was coming over, so he'd better get started on his famous baked mac and cheese with the crispy goodness on top—her favorite.

"I'm way ahead of both of you," he said, lifting the lid off a steaming pot of macaroni, ready to be drained.

Ten minutes later, Sal buzzed to say Rebecca was on her way up. I don't know why he bothers. She practically lives here.

When I opened the door, Rebecca was sucking on a huge iced caramel mocha frappé. I gave her my best gagging face.

"I'm carbo loading for basketball tomorrow," she explained.

"I don't think it works that way. That thing is mostly sugar, no complex carbs. Besides, if you're going to drink all those calories, have a shake. It tastes better. Plus, that caffeine'll kill you."

Rebecca shrugged and went back to slurping her drink.

"Hello, Miss Becky," said Daddy. He's the only one who calls her Becky. Even to her own parents, she's Rebecca.

"Hey, J.F.," said Rebecca, because she can never bring herself to call him Joshua, like he asked her to. She sniffed the air. "Speaking of complex carbs, is that my mac and cheese?"

"It just went in the oven. I'll call you girls when it's ready."

"Let's go say hi to Mr. Elephant," Rebecca said, meaning the little statue of Ganesha, the elephant-headed Hindu god Nanaji had given me.

I poured myself a glass of water, and we went to my room. The first thing Rebecca did was rub Ganesha's belly, because I once told her it brings good luck, and money. At least that's what Nanaji had told me. He used to keep it on a little altar that I'd replicated as well as I could on top of my dresser, next to a small brass bowl of *teeka* made from turmeric and incense ashes that I'd shmear on its head just the way he used to do. For me, it wasn't a religious thing. Just a little ritual to remember him by. I did it now.

I used to love it when Nanaji came to visit us. He was like a giant kid when he came to New York, and he loved to explore. He marveled how the drivers didn't lean on their horns, and how everyone stayed in their own lane—the smaller cars and cycles didn't try to squeeze in between the larger, slower vehicles. Only Nanaji would think New York drivers are polite.

He loved Central Park best. He would swing me to his shoulders and walk the four blocks to the park, stopping to buy peeled mangoes on a stick or coconut ices from the Latina ladies along the way. Inside the park he would point out the trees bearing edible fruit, and it was my job to reach up and pick some, then feed them to him one at a time as we strolled across the grassy fields. We were never hungry for dinner when we came home.

I knew he would have liked my sari idea.

I ran it past Rebecca now, but she seemed skeptical.

"I don't know," she said, draping the fabric over her arm. "I mean, it's so pretty, but . . ."

"But what?"

"Nothing, it's just—different, you know?"

"That's the point!" I said. Rebecca and Mum can both be so exasperatingly conformist.

Then Rebecca had an idea: "Why don't I go with you guys next time?"

"Why, so you and Mum can gang up on me? Thanks but no thanks." Rebecca was way too preppy for my taste. Today, for example, she wore a striped oxford under a royal blue V-neck, dark skinny jeans, and black leather basketball shoes—on a *Sunday*. She looked like an ad for a country club.

"Fine," she said, changing the subject. "Let's play Bollywood movie."

"Okay," I said, relieved. I gathered up the usual assort-ment of accessories—colored glass bangles, jingle-bell toe rings, silk scarves, stick-on rhinestone-and-velvet *bindis*—while Rebecca kicked off her shoes and popped in the CD. We pretended we were dancing in the rain, winding our-selves in the sari and then spinning free. For the full effect, I broke off a generous hunk of sandalwood incense from the stash I'd taken from my cousin Vijay, kneaded it into a tall pyramid, and buried the base in the brass *teeka* bowl. After I lit it, I opened the window a crack to keep the smoky san-dalwood smell from wandering into the hallway, since tech-nically I'm not allowed to use incense, or anything requiring matches, in my room. Luckily, though, Daddy had burned something in the kitchen, so no one was the wiser. That crispy top gets him every time.

Rebecca and I took turns playing the heroine, and the villain behind the tree. When it was her turn to be the villain, I drew a thin mustache on her upper lip, using Mum's old mascara wand. We were cracking ourselves up pretty hard.

"Nahee! Nahee!" I cried, whenever Rebecca-as-villain caught me. "No! No!"

"Bwa-ha-ha!" Rebecca replied, more horror movie than Bollywood musical, but it didn't matter. She yanked the free edge of the sari, sending me spinning like a top. Then it was her turn to be the heroine, even though she still had the mascara mustache. I wrapped her in the sari, arms and all. She looked like a silk burrito with just her head sticking out, her baby-fine reddish brown hair flying in all directions. Her hair was practically standing on end from static. I yanked the free end of the sari to give her a good spin. She reeled into my dresser, snagging the sari on the edge of the top drawer, and for a second we thought we'd ripped it. I unwound her slowly to inspect it, but it was fine. Thunder rumbled in the distance.

"That was close," she said, smoothing down her hair.

What happened next was like that dream where you can see disaster coming from a mile away, but you're powerless to stop it or even scream. The wind kicked up outside, blowing the window shade inward. Rebecca reached out to keep it from knocking everything off my dresser, accidentally brushing against the smoldering pyramid of incense. She yelped and pulled her arm back, sending both Ganesha and the *teeka* bowl—ashes, turmeric, glowing incense, and everything—tumbling down. I snatched frantically at the air, not even caring if I burned myself, but I was too late. The incense had landed, smoldering side down, on the sari, burning a large, incense-shaped hole in the fine silk. Rebecca threw her drink on it.

"What are you doing?" I yelled. "I had water."

"Reflex!" Rebecca said. "I wasn't thinking."

"Lunch!" Daddy called from the kitchen.

I picked up the incense carefully and plopped it in the glass of water, where it fizzled out. Then I turned off the CD player and gave Rebecca one of the makeup towelettes to wipe off the mascara mustache while I stashed the ruined sari under my pillow, caramel mocha frappé and all.

"Did you burn yourself?" I asked.

Rebecca shook her head. She looked like she wanted to say something else, but I put out my hand.

"DON'T say anything—I need to think."

"I'm really sorry," she whispered.

"It's not your fault," I said, opening the door and pulling her through it. "Now go out there and act natural."

Lunch was pretty gloomy. Mum was already irritated by our disaster of a shopping trip, so luckily she didn't notice Rebecca and me staring mutely at our plates. But Daddy did.

"Why is everyone so quiet?" he asked, looking from Mum to me to Rebecca. "Did someone die while I was burning lunch?"

At the word "burning," Rebecca jumped, dropping her fork. Daddy can be kind of clueless, but this time I was glad.

"Don't be morbid, Joshua," said Mum.

"More, Miss Becky?" Daddy offered, even though Rebecca had barely touched what was on her plate. "You can scrape the burned stuff off."

"No, thanks, J.F.," Rebecca mumbled, avoiding his eyes. "I have to go home—um, basketball practice."

Chapter 9

Rebecca and I started our bat mitzvah lessons Monday after school. Mine was first.

Since it wasn't a regular Hebrew school day, just a one-on-one lesson, Rabbi Aron was wearing faded jeans and a flannel shirt, which seemed kind of weird to me. I mean, I guess rabbis are the same as other people, but still.

"You seemed a little distracted in class last week, Tara," he said. I blushed, hoping he hadn't witnessed me and Sheila Rosenberg fighting after all. I nodded. "Is there something you'd like to talk to me about?"

Sometimes I get the feeling he knows more than he lets on.

"Rabbi Aron, can I ask you a question?"

"Anything, Tara."

"Sheila Rosenberg says I'm not Jewish," I said.

Rabbi put down his pen and folded his thick, freckled hands on the desk. "And why would she say that, Tara Feinstein?"

"She says because my mother isn't Jewish—but she is."

Rabbi smiled. "I know that, Tara," he said.

"But—"

"Let me ask you something: Are you Jewish?"

"That's what I wanted to ask you," I said, relieved.

"*Bubeleh*," he said, "you're Jewish. No one can take that from you. I'm asking you how you *feel*. In your heart."

"How is being Jewish *supposed* to make my heart feel?"

"Oy, Tara." Rabbi chuckled. "Who but a Jew answers a question with another question?"

I didn't know whether I was supposed to answer that or not, so I kept quiet. Somehow, though, I felt a little bit better.

"Shall we look at your *haftarah* now?" he asked, referring to the special reading I would chant at my bat mitzvah. I was supposed to have studied it over the summer, but that had never really happened. I'd been cramming for the last two weeks, trying to catch up, but I still wasn't quite ready for an in-depth discussion, so I was glad when Rabbi asked, "Is something else troubling you, Tara?"

I hesitated. There were several things I wanted to ask him: about God, and religion, and maybe some practical advice on how to tell Mum about the sari. I decided to start with that.

"It's nothing," I said. "Only, I kind of did a bad thing."

"How bad?"

"Not on *purpose*. I, like, accidentally—I mean, I broke

something, or—something. And I'm afraid to tell my mother."

"Something of hers?"

"No, it's mine. But it's something very special and old. And probably expensive."

"You don't want to tell me what it is?" Rabbi asked. I shook my head. "Is there another adult you can talk to?"

"No," I said. "Just Gran."

Rabbi seemed to be suppressing a smile. "And what would your grandmother say?"

"I don't know." I shrugged.

Rabbi raised his eyebrows in disbelief. "Wouldn't she say you ought to come clean—tell your mother what happened?"

"Probably not," I said. "They're not exactly besties."

Rabbi chuckled. "All right, what do *you* think the right answer is, Tara?"

"I know I need to tell her," I said to the floor. What I really wanted to know was *how*.

"Are you worried she'll be angry?" Rabbi asked.

"I know she'll be angry," I said. "I can handle that."

"Then what is it?"

"I'm afraid . . . she'll be . . ." I fished around for the right word, the right feeling. All at once it came to me: "Disappointed."

"Aha!" said Rabbi. He sounded rather cheerful. I raised an eyebrow. "Now we're getting somewhere."

"We are?"

"You're afraid of how this . . . accident reflects on you as a human being, yes? That's a bit out of proportion to the crime, isn't it?"

"I don't know," I whispered. After all, there was the wrath of Meena Auntie to be reckoned with. The thought made me shiver.

Meena Auntie was terrifying. One time when I was little, she said she wanted to eat me up, and I believed her.

"She doesn't mean it," Mum had assured me.

"Oh, but I do, Rita," Meena Auntie teased.

"Not *literally*," Mum said, glaring at her older sister.

"Mumma's gonna eat-choo, Mumma's gonna eat-choo," Vijay sang, and Meena Auntie smacked him on the side of his head. That's why Vijay is a pothead now.

"Tara, you're a very mature young lady. Whatever happened was, as you say, an accident. Tell your mother the truth. Don't let it hang over your head. You have more important things to think about—your *haftarah*, for example."

After that, there was no more stalling. I flipped open the study guide, and we got to work.

Later, on the way out, I bumped straight into Sheila Rosenberg and her mother. I bet they didn't have any secrets from each other.

Rebecca was still sitting on the steps outside. "Your turn," I said. "Except I saw Sheila and her mom by Rabbi's office."

"I know. Mrs. R needs to talk to him about some kind of special *aliyah* for her uncle Walter. He had a stroke."

I was too distracted by my own problems to spend time wondering why she knew that much inside information about the Rosenberg family. Rabbi was right: I had to tell Mum the truth. Just get it over with. Caught up in my own thoughts, I turned to leave.

"Hey! Aren't you going to wait for me?" Rebecca asked in surprise.

"Can't today. I have to go straight home."

Her face fell. "You're mad at me."

"I'm not *mad*. I just need to talk to Mum."

Rebecca had an idea. "Want me to tell her? I mean, it was my fault."

"It wasn't," I said, getting exasperated.

"Okay," she said in a small voice. "Call me later?"

"I will."

"Tara—good luck."

"Thanks," I said. "I'll need it."

Chapter 10

All during dinner, I practiced in my head. I had decided to go with the direct approach. Just tell her what happened, beg forgiveness, and move on. Maybe I'd be grounded, but I didn't care. It couldn't be worse than this guilt.

After dinner, Mum gave Daddy a quick kiss on the cheek and went back to her office to finish her latest proposal, while I loaded the dishwasher. Then I rehearsed one more time, pacing restlessly in my room.

"Don't let it hang over your head," Rabbi had said. It was time to stop stalling. I knocked softly on her office door.

"It's open," she called.

I swallowed hard. "Mum, I need to talk to you. About the sari."

Mum turned away from the screen and took off her glasses to look at me.

"I've been meaning to talk to you, too, Tara," she said. "I've been thinking, and if you really want to wear it, it's okay with me."

"I—wait, what?" I said.

"Your bas mitzvah is your initiation into adulthood," she said. "If you want to express yourself by wearing a sari, who am I to say no?"

I didn't know what to say. I mean, probably she was just sick of shopping with me, but still—

"You're going to need practice—and lots of safety pins," Mum said. She glanced wistfully at the jumble of family pictures pinned on the wall next to her desk, placing her forefinger on the one of herself and Meena Auntie at their aunt Sarita's wedding in Delhi. Mum was maybe nine years old, looking stiff and frightened in her first formal sari—electric blue, in a shiny-looking synthetic fabric. Meena stood by her side, already looking like an adult at nineteen. I hadn't noticed it before, but in the picture Meena was wearing the black and crimson silk sari. My sari. The one I had ruined. I felt sick to my stomach. I wanted to throw up.

All I wanted was to be allowed to be different in a good way, and for Mum to understand. To be myself, on my own terms, and not have that be weird. To stand out and fit in at the same time. A normal Jewish kid—with a healthy sprinkling of *masala* on top. To my surprise, she had gotten the point after all. But now I'd ruined everything.

So I didn't tell Mum the truth about the sari. I couldn't. There was only one adult I could talk to, and even she probably wouldn't be able to help. But I had nowhere else to turn. I went back to my room, took a deep breath, and picked up the phone.

Chapter 11

he next day, after school, I heard the elevator ding on our floor, and I didn't wait. I flung the door open and collapsed into Gran's arms.

"Thank God you're here!" I gasped. "I have Hebrew in forty-five minutes, so hurry."

"What was so important I had to miss bingo?" she asked, undoing the strings of her rain bonnet. Mum was out at a client meeting and Daddy was grading papers at school, so the coast was clear. Without another word, I grabbed Gran's hand and led her to my room. I got the cedar box out from under the dresser and put it on my bed.

"What's this?"

"Open it," I said.

Gran put on her half-moon glasses and opened the box. She peered inside at the sari.

"There's been an accident," I said.

"What kind of an accident?"

I hurriedly summarized what had happened when Rebecca came over on Sunday, hoping I could leave out the part about the incense.

Gran lifted out the ruined sari to examine it up close. Bits of frayed silk stuck to her hand, along with a gob of half-dried caramel sauce. She grimaced. "Perhaps you ought to start from the beginning," she said.

"Okay, see—me and Rebecca—"

"Rebecca and I . . ."

"Right, Rebecca and I were playing Bollywood movie, see? You know?" Clearly she didn't know. "Pretending to dance in the rain and all that? Anyway, that's how it happened."

Gran sniffed it and wrinkled her nose. "Why does it smell like smoke?" she asked, giving me a sharp look.

"Because . . ." I mumbled, "we lit incense."

"Speak up!"

"It got burned."

"Aha!" Gran squawked. "I ought to wring your neck, playing with matches."

"Incense," I corrected her.

"Don't be fresh. Tell me again why it's all sticky?"

I'd called Gran because she'd know what to *do*. But all at once I wished Nani—my other grandmother—were there. She would have understood how I *felt*, how important the sari was. While Mum and Auntie would be furious, Nani would have had some crazy ritual that would make me feel better. Maybe wave an onion around and then bury it in a flowerpot to banish the evil spirits responsible for the damage. Start over with a clean slate. None of that mattered unless it really could be fixed, though.

"Rebecca threw her drink on it, which happened to be a caramel mocha frappé."

"Brilliant," said Gran. She looked over the sari section by section, taking in the whole charred, sticky, coffee-and-smoke-smelling, turmeric-and-ash-stained mess.

"It wasn't her best moment," I admitted. "But now my sari is ruined! And Mum is going to kill me. After Meena Auntie kills her."

"You mean your mother doesn't know?"

I shook my head. Gran brightened.

"Can you fix it?" I asked in a small voice.

"First we have to wash it. You'll be lucky if this gunk hasn't already set in completely. Come on. Bring the Ivory Snow."

I was so happy she was taking charge that I didn't even mind her being mad at me. Gran rinsed the sari in the bathroom sink while I went rummaging in the linen closet for the laundry soap.

"Pour some in here. Not that much. Half a cup. That's it." Gran swished the sari around gently, squeezing the soap through the fabric, concentrating on the coffee stains and the sticky bits. I tried to help. "Don't *rub* it, Tara, or the material will fray. Leave this to me." I sat down on the toilet-seat lid.

Gran paused and looked at me for a long moment. Something softened in her eyes.

"You should have told your mother, you know."

"I know."

"She deserves more credit than you give her." I'd never heard Gran sound so sympathetic toward Mum. I was surprised. "Your mother may give me *tsuris*, but she has a good heart. Don't break it."

"By ruining the sari?"

"No, *meshuggeneh*," she said, splashing me with soapy water. "For shutting her out. Think about it."

Of course she was right. I was so caught up in my own guilt, I hadn't really given any thought to how Mum was going to feel. I mean, I knew she'd be *mad*—but I hadn't considered that she might also be *hurt*.

"So what do we do now?"

"Oh, it's *we* now, is it? Well—*I* am going to take it home to dry, and then we'll see what's what," Gran said, wringing out the sopping wet silk. She grabbed a clean towel from the shelf under the sink and rolled the sari in it, then crammed the whole thing into her enormous purse.

We walked back to the living room. It was 4:10. I was going to have to run all the way to Hebrew school to get there on time. Gran was taking forever putting on her coat and rain bonnet.

"Go," she said, dismissing me with a wave. "I'll lock up."

"You're my hero, Gran," I said, hugging her.

"Crazy kid," she muttered.

I was out of breath when I arrived at Hebrew school, just three minutes before class started. Rebecca was waiting for me outside the classroom, looking nervous.

"How'd it go?"

"Don't worry," I said. "Gran can fix it. Gran can fix anything."

I sounded a lot more confident than I felt.

Chapter 12

After Robotics Club on Wednesday, I waited in the hall while Ben-o was cleaning up his worktable. I felt like we hadn't talked in ages, now that I had private bat mitzvah lessons once a week, plus Hebrew school Tuesday and Thursday afternoons and an hour on Sunday mornings. That was the killer—waking up on Sundays for no good reason. Rebecca also had basketball and dance class. I wondered how she managed all that. Ben-o had chess and Robotics, but that was all.

Mum had wanted me to give up Robotics, but I persuaded her that I could do Hebrew school and Robotics and get all my homework done and not burn out the way my cousin Vijay had in seventh grade and never recovered. It didn't leave me much time for my friends, though. If it weren't for Robotics, I'd barely get to see Ben-o at all, other than walking to school in the morning. I was kind of missing him.

"Do you want to come over and play Stingray?" I asked hopefully, when he came out into the hall.

"Can't. I already have plans," he said.

"Oh. With who?"

"With Adam. Wanna shoot some hoops with us in the park?" he offered.

"You're playing basketball with the shortest boy in the seventh grade?" I snickered.

"Don't be mean."

"I wasn't," I said. "I was just kidding." Actually, Adam wasn't half bad without Ryan, so I said I would join them.

"Cool," said Ben-o. "Adam's getting his probation form signed by Mr. H. I told him I'd wait and walk over together."

But when Adam came out, Ryan was with him. I rolled my eyes meaningfully at Ben-o.

"Ready to play ball?" said Ryan.

Ben-o seemed as surprised as I was. His lip curled in a sneer. "Whatever," he said.

Ryan talked nonstop on the way to the park, regaling Adam with a dumb story about Hebrew school the day before, which Adam had apparently missed.

"So Jacobson goes, 'Moses and Judah Maccabee had a lot in common. Does anyone know why?' and I'm like, 'They both had big noses?' And she's like, 'It's stuff like that . . .'" Ryan paused. "What's it called? You know, when all the Jews were killed?"

"Um, the *Holocaust*?" I offered.

Ryan continued. "And Jacobson's like, 'It's stuff like that

that caused the Holocaust.' And I'm like, 'Really, the Holocaust happened because of big-nose comments?' And she's like—"

"That's offensive on so many levels," I said.

By the time we reached the park, Ryan had switched gears and was complaining about how "stupid" Robotics Club was, which really got under Ben-o's skin.

"So why are you in it?" Ben-o asked.

"You know why," Ryan said, trying for a layup and missing. Ben-o got the ball. "If I get suspended, my mom is going to send me to military school."

"I mean, why this club?" Ben-o insisted. "Why Robotics?"

Ryan shrugged and actually blushed a little. Ben-o did an overhead pass to me that Ryan intercepted.

"Thought so," Ben-o said.

"What?" said Adam, looking as confused as I felt. I kept looking from Ben-o to Ryan, trying to figure out what this was about. Was Ben-o back on *that* again?

"Yeah, Ben-o, what?" I asked, weary of the guessing game.

"What's wrong, Benny?" Ryan teased. "Can't stand a little competition?"

Ben-o laughed hollowly. "Competition?" he sneered, pausing to make an easy basket. I got the ball and dribbled it past Adam, who tried, and failed, to steal it midbounce. "Do you mean in Robotics? Or basketball? Or are you talking about Tara?"

I stopped dribbling and held the ball, staring at Ben-o. I was beginning to get the idea that this wasn't so much about Ryan. That it was somehow about us—Ben-o and me.

I thrust the ball at him, maybe a little too hard, fed up with trying to figure out what was eating him. What did he care if Ryan liked me? That was my bad luck, not his. Was he jealous? As if I could be friends, let alone best friends, with Ryan Berger. *Please*. It didn't make sense. Unless . . .

"I gotta go," Ben-o said, throwing Ryan a blind pass while looking at me. "See ya, Tara."

Was he really leaving me in the park with them? After dropping that bomb?

"Giving up so easily?" Ryan gloated.

"Shut up, Berger," I snapped. "Go ruin someone else's life."

"Hey!" said Adam. "Where's everyone going?"

"Wait up, Ben-o!" I called, running after him. But he didn't stop. He grabbed his skateboard from under the bench and took off. I couldn't catch up.

Chapter 13

Almost a week went by, during which Ben-o avoided being alone with me. We didn't even have movie night on Saturday, because he had to pick up building supplies with his dad and didn't get home until almost ten.

On Monday morning, he acted as if nothing had happened, so I decided not to bring it up in the five minutes we had before we met up with Rebecca. I had other things on my mind, like whether or not I'd ruined a priceless heirloom sari.

* * *

Monday afternoon, after my bat mitzvah lesson, Gran brought over the dry and freshly ironed sari. Mum was at yet another client meeting, so we had the living room to ourselves. Gran had done a great job. The coffee and turmeric stains were barely visible on the darker parts of the fabric, but, of course, there were still the frizzle-edged burn holes.

"Well," said Gran, "I wish I could say 'good as new,' but we'll have to make the best of it."

She held the sari up against me, rearranging the fabric this way and that. Then she shook her head and offered her professional opinion: "No matter which way you wrap it, the holes are going to show." Seeing my face, though, she said, "Don't give up yet," draping the fabric over my shoulder. "We could still find a solution. Hold this." She handed one end of the sari to me, then gathered up some of the fabric behind me, stuffing it into the back of my pants. "Stay still. Now turn toward me. Don't move . . . A little to the right . . . Now lift your left arm. Other left," she said when I automatically lifted my right arm.

"This isn't going to work," I said.

"Maybe if I cut it down the middle."

I shook my head. "It'll never work. I can't wear half a sari. You have to have something to tuck in."

Gran snapped her fingers. "I know! This is the perfect job for Marvin."

"Can he fix it?" I wondered.

"You know the expression 'Life hands you lemons, make lemonade'?"

"No," I said.

"Well, when life hands you a *shmatta*—a rag—you make a new dress."

I threw myself at her gratefully. "Gran! That's the best idea you've ever had."

"Well," she said, straightening her hair. "Marvin's

shomer Shabbos, so we'll have to go on Sunday. Be ready at nine. We don't want to arouse any suspicions."

"But I have Hebrew school on Sunday."

"That's your cover story right there," Gran said.

Just then, we heard a key in the lock, and Meena Auntie and Vijay barged in. Was it normal that both my grandmother and my aunt had keys? I wished Sal would announce them the way he announces Rebecca every single time she comes over—sometimes even twice a day. But Sal is afraid of Meena Auntie, and Gran, too, I think.

I quickly shoved the sari under the couch.

"Meen-a-la," Gran cried, flinging out her arms. She kicked me lightly to let me know that the sari was still visible beneath the couch. I jammed it farther back with my foot before anyone else noticed.

"Ruthie-jee!" Meena Auntie replied, gathering Gran in her ample embrace.

"Somebody's had her hair done," Gran sang. For some reason, the two of them got along great. Probably because they both knew it irritated Mum.

Meena Auntie is ten years older than Mum and still dyes her hair black. She goes to the same salon as Gran, except not every single week, and Auntie washes her own hair at home on a regular basis. She always stops by here after the salon.

"Do you like it, Ruthie-jee?" she asked, cupping the loose curls in the palm of her hand. "I've had a double process." Whatever that was.

"On you it looks good," Gran said, patting Meena Auntie's cheek.

Vijay plopped down on the couch next to me. He was still wearing the *rakhi* bracelet I gave him in August. I make him one every year. Raksha Bandhan, or Rakhi, is this Indian holiday where a sister ties a decorative cord—a *rakhi*—on her brother's wrist to symbolically protect him from evil. The brother gives his sister a gift in return, usually money, and promises his lifetime protection of her. If you don't have a brother, any boy cousin will do, which is where Vijay came in.

I guess it didn't work all that well, since Vijay was constantly up to no good. And I didn't know what kind of trouble he could protect me from, but it was nice to have a brother at least once a year. He'd always been a pretty good sport about it, too, even though I made his bracelets really silly-looking on purpose. "Yo, homie," I heard him tell his friend Arjun once, "check out what my girl Tara gave me." Another time, when Arjun and Biff made fun of him for all the tinsel and beads, he said, "Don't hate me just 'cause my sister love me, bro." After that, I made them more and more outrageous every year, with big dumb felt flowers and glitter and rhinestones, just to hear Vijay call me his sister. As an added bonus, Meena Auntie always made sure he gave me money like he was supposed to. In previous years, when she used to give him the money to give me, he'd been known to skim off the top, but last year he gave me almost a hundred dollars in small bills from his own pocket. I didn't even want to know where he got that kind of money.

I used to wish I had a real brother—preferably an older one—or, if not that, then a little sister to look up to me. I would teach her to build robots and shoot hoops and make sure she never, ever had to wear a dress. Unless she wanted to.

Mum came home, and Gran left to finish her grocery shopping. Meena Auntie followed Mum into her office. Vijay waited until she was gone.

"Cuz, I gotta *ax* you something," he said, twisting this year's *rakhi* on his wrist—a rather understated silver macramé embellished with tiny jingle bells and red fun fur. "You know your bazmatzah thing?"

"Bat *mitzvah*," I corrected him. "And it's *ask*, Vijay, not *ax*. Meena Auntie would smack you if she heard you talk like that."

"Yeah," he agreed, rubbing his head. "Anyway, I was wondering if—"

"Forget it."

"What? I ain't even asked you yet."

"You want to be my deejay," I said. "Forget it."

"Why you gotta be like that, shorty?"

"Be like what? I know all about DJ Vijay. Do you own any records from this millennium?"

"You got something against 'Billie Jean'?"

"Veej, that song is older than you are."

"It's what the people want." He shrugged. "Listen, shorts, if I promise to play what your peeps want to hear, can I get the gig?"

Truthfully, I didn't care all that much. I mean, I hadn't been consulted on anything else of importance, so . . .

"Ask Mum," I said bitterly. "She's making all the decisions."

"Come on," he pleaded. "You ask. You know I ain't got no creds." (This because of the peanut M&M's he sold to Mum's book group as a "fund-raiser" last year—the "fund" being Vijay and Biff's pockets.)

"Ask her yourself," I said firmly. "I've got my own problems." And I certainly wasn't going to cash in my chips for this.

Vijay perked up. "Problems? Like what? Maybe we could help each other."

"I don't think so, Vijay, unless . . ." I stopped. Unless what? Unless Vijay learned to sew? Unless he took the blame for ruining the sari? "Never mind," I said, knowing that anything I said to him could and would be used against me someday. Besides, he really couldn't afford to get smacked in the head anymore.

"Did perfect little Tara do something wrong?" Vijay wheedled, still fiddling with the rakhi cord on his wrist. "Tell it to me, cuz. I'm here for you."

Without meaning to, I glanced down and saw a corner of the sari still sticking out from beneath the couch. I tried casually to push it back some more with my foot, but Vijay noticed.

"What have we here?" he said, pulling the sari out. When he saw what had happened to it, his eyes got wide. "Dude," he said, "you're toast." He turned to look at me gravely, and then he burst out laughing like a demented hyena, pointing at me and clutching his stomach. "Bah-ha-ha! Busted!" He couldn't seem to believe his luck at my misfortune. "Tara's in truh-uh-ble." His eyes lit up like neon dollar signs.

"Shut it," I hissed, snatching back the sari and rolling it into a ball.

"Vijayyyyyii!" Meena Auntie yelled, sticking her head out the door of Mum's office. "What is happening out there?"

"Nothing, Mataji," Vijay called back in a high falsetto, cracking himself up again.

"Stop aggravating your cousin."

Vijay turned to me with a cunning smile. "You know what this means, don't you?" He did an exaggerated *bhangra* dance move, turning his palms toward the ceiling as if he were balancing a heavy tray in each hand while rhythmically pumping his shoulders up and down to the beat of an imaginary *dhol* drum. *"Hoi, hoi, hoi!"*

"Whatever." I sighed, stuffing the balled-up sari under the couch again. "You breathe one single word about this and the deal is off—*and* I'll tell Meena Auntie what really happened to her cobalt vase."

He shrugged happily. "Can I tell Rita Auntie you practically begged me to deejay?"

"You will anyway."

"Yeah," he agreed.

"Whatever," I said again. "But listen—I'll give you a list

of songs to play. You just play them. No Michael Jackson, no Kool and the Gang, definitely no Sinatra. You've got to promise."

"Not even 'Celebration'?"

I shook my head vigorously.

"'New York, New York'?"

"Not even once," I warned.

"Hip-hop?"

"Fine, but nothing more than three years old."

"A'ight. A'ight. I'm hearin' ya."

"Seriously, Vijay? You're such a poser."

"Yeah, well, good luck with that," he said, indicating the sari. "You're gonna need it."

Mum walked Meena Auntie to the living room, a trick she uses when she wants her to leave. Meena Auntie took the hint.

"*Chalo, beta,*" she said to Vijay. "He will be waiting."

"He" meant Aravind Uncle, her husband. They didn't speak to each other. I don't mean they were getting divorced or anything. They were together; they just didn't talk. Meena Auntie didn't even like to say his name.

The only thing they actually argued about was the reason they weren't on speaking terms in the first place. Everyone knew Uncle was dying to move back to India, where it's warm and the food is familiar and all the men chew *paan* and have small mustaches like his. Meena Auntie won't live anywhere but her "Amreeka"—certainly not India. It's a mystery why he didn't just go back without her.

Auntie was hard to figure out. On the one hand, she was ferociously patriotic and wouldn't trade her U.S. citizenship for anything, but she was also much more "Indian" than Mum. Like, Mum wouldn't be caught dead in a *salwar kameez*, which is what Auntie wore every day except when she had to appear in court to defend a client. Mum said Auntie turned America into her own little India instead of assimilating. Auntie said where else but in America could you have the freedom to do that? Which was a good point. Besides, it was hard for me to imagine Aravind Uncle being happy anywhere.

He wasn't even happy the last time we all went to India. I remember him standing around glumly in Nani and Nanaji's garden, wearing a gray woolen cap even though it was like seventy degrees outside. He stood with his hands clasped behind his back, staring absently through the wrought-iron bars of the car gate, watching the life outside the little compound—the *chaiwallah* selling steamy tea in clay cups, the wandering ear-piercer, a pack of filthy puppies sucking on their mother's underside in the dirt road. A bored cow batted her tail at the flies circling her behind and munched on the charred trash at the corner, not bothering to pick out the paper bags from the fruit rinds.

Auntie had followed his gaze and snorted. Just moments before, Daddy had plugged up the toilet again, for like the third time, and she was still ranting about the state of plumbing and hygiene in India.

"This is your precious India, *haan*?" she said, turning viciously on Aravind Uncle. "Dysentery. Third-world plumbing. This is your paradise."

Uncle had looked right through her, without saying a word.

Now, while Auntie put on her raincoat, Vijay turned to me once more, doing his *bhangra* moves as if to remind me of my promise. I shot him back a menacing look to remind him of his.

"Rita Auntie," Vijay said, with wide-eyed, blinking innocence, "Tara here was just begging me to deejay at her bazmatzah—"

"Bat *mitzvah*," I spat.

"Begging you?" Mum said, skeptical. I shrugged and looked out the window.

"What a lovely gesture," Auntie said. "Vijay would be honored, won't you, *beta*?"

"Of course," Vijay said, smirking.

"Well," said Mum, "if that's what you want, Tara, I don't see why not."

I thought, *Really—you don't see why not?* Because I could think of a reason or two. I didn't *mind* having him deejay, as long as he stuck to my rules. It's just that she agreed so easily, after nitpicking *me* about every little detail. She didn't even stop to consider that he might show up late or not at all or that he might play something inappropriate, like hardcore. He might do any of those things. It was as if she wasn't even paying attention anymore. I wished she had half as much faith in me as she seemed to have in him. Not that he'd even earned it.

Chapter 14

I was waiting at the door for Gran when she arrived Sunday morning.

"What are you two plotting?" Daddy asked when he saw us whispering.

"Who's plotting?" Gran answered, shoving the sari into her enormous purse once more. "Can't I take my only granddaughter out for breakfast on a Sunday?"

Daddy raised an eyebrow. "Tara, don't you have Hebrew school at ten? It's already nine fifteen."

"Oh, look who learned to tell time," said Gran.

"Ma—" Daddy began, then changed his mind. "Have a good time. Just get Tara to Hebrew school on time. Don't get her into any trouble."

"Who's making trouble?" Gran replied.

We took two trains downtown, then walked about seven blocks to Marvin's shop, Eisenman and Bergstein's Embroidery and Finishing. The shop gate was rolled halfway down. I had to stoop down to get inside, but Gran barely had to duck.

"Knock, knock!" she called. "Ah, there's my Marvin."

Marvin's really nice. He has the same kind face and light green eyes as Daddy, only he's ten years older and has a fuzzy reddish beard. He also wears a *yarmulke* at all times, not just in temple.

"So, Aunt Ruth," he said, clasping his hands, "let's see it."

Gran pulled the sari out of her purse and spread it on Marvin's cutting table, explaining all the while. She shook her fist at me when she got to the part about the incense.

Marvin admired the fabric silently for a long time, rubbing the substantial silk between his thumb and forefinger, nodding along as Gran spoke. "A fine material like this, I could really do something," he said after a long pause.

"That's my Marvin," said Gran, pinching him hard on the cheek even though he's a grown-up.

Marvin and Gran discussed the dress details at length. I tuned them out completely, playing with the pinking shears and the little scraps of fabric that were everywhere. Then Marvin came at me with a tape measure and jotted down some notes. They both seemed satisfied with the plan.

"Well?" said Gran.

"Leave it to me, Aunt Ruth."

"With the leftovers, you'll make me a cushion," she added.

Great. Gran's couch and I would have matching outfits.

"I'll try, Aunt Ruth, but I doubt there will be much left." Marvin winked at me, and I smiled.

"Don't do anything yet, Marvin dear," Gran said, rolling

up the sari and stashing it back in her purse. "First we have to break the news to Rita."

That was the part I'd been dreading. I stopped smiling.

✳ ✳ ✳

We took a taxi back uptown. Gran had the driver drop me off near the synagogue, as part of my alibi. I got there just as Hebrew school was letting out. Rebecca was on the steps talking to Sheila Rosenberg when I walked up.

"Hey," I said.

"Hey," said Rebecca. "How'd it go?"

"Good, I think. Marvin's going to make me a dress."

Rebecca seemed truly relieved. Sheila just looked from one to the other of us, bewildered.

"You cut Hebrew school to go *shopping*?"

"I wasn't cutting," I said. "Or shopping. I was with my grandmother."

"Rabbi was asking where you were."

"Why would he ask you?"

"Not me," said Sheila. "Rebecca."

"What did you say?" I asked, turning to Rebecca.

Rebecca shrugged. "Nothing. I said I didn't know."

"I don't think he believed you," said Sheila.

"Well, it's technically true," Rebecca said.

When we got to Sheila's corner, she didn't cross the street right away.

"What are you guys doing today?" she asked, more to Rebecca than me.

"Studying," I answered for her. "We have an English quiz tomorrow. Why?"

"No reason." She shrugged. "I thought maybe we could hang out."

Seriously? I caught Rebecca's eye with a look that said *I'll handle this.* "You're not in our class," I pointed out matter-of-factly. Rebecca looked embarrassed.

"It's okay," Sheila said. "Another time."

"Another time," Rebecca echoed.

"What was *that* about?" I asked after Sheila left.

"Nothing," Rebecca scolded. "You don't have to be so blatantly rude to her."

"Whatever," I said. Rebecca can be a bit too neutral sometimes.

Rebecca went home to get her English book. I walked the rest of the way home by myself.

"You make it to Hebrew school today?" asked Daddy.

"Yeah," I said—which, as Rebecca would say, was "technically true." I neglected to mention that Hebrew school was over by the time I got there.

"Hmm," said Daddy, still vaguely suspicious. "Where's Rebecca?"

"She went home to get her English book. We have a quiz tomorrow." As if on cue, the doorman buzzed.

＊ ＊ ＊

Rebecca and I made ourselves a power snack of peanut butter and celery. Then I spent about a half hour drilling her on the parts of speech until she stopped mixing up her adverbs and adjectives. Next, we turned to our bat mitzvah readings, because Rebecca said that Rabbi wanted us to bring discussion topics to Monday's lesson.

Rebecca's Torah portion was Mishpatim—the one about Jewish laws, all the "eye for an eye, tooth for a tooth" stuff and how to punish a bull if it gores someone. I didn't get why that was a law, when bulls couldn't even read. I also noticed that a lot of the laws were negatives: don't do this and don't do that. It sounded a lot like Mum, actually.

Here's the part that blew my mind, though: Jews owned *slaves*. I'm not kidding. *Jewish* slaves. The *parashah* starts with all the rules about how to treat your slaves, such as not hitting them with a rod and letting them go free after seven years. I was stunned.

"I know, right?" said Rebecca. "I couldn't believe it either, the first time I read it."

"But—what are you going to do with that?"

"Like in my speech, you mean? Find a lesson in it," she said, in a pretty good Rabbi Aron imitation, deep, gravelly voice and all.

"I'm *serious*," I said. "How can you even joke about it?"

"I *am* serious. There's got to be a good explanation, right?"

"I hope so." But what could that explanation be? Those were exactly the kinds of contradictions that had started me wondering if I believed in God in the first place.

I flopped down across the bed. "Rebecca, do you believe in God?" I asked her, staring at the ceiling.

"Is that your discussion topic?" Rebecca asked, alarmed.

"Of course not. Just—do you?"

"This is getting way too heavy, T. Can I at least finish my snack first?" *Crunch, crunch.*

"I'm serious," I said again. "Why is it such a hard question?"

Rebecca licked a glob of peanut butter from her lip. "Yes."

"Yes, it's a hard question?"

"*Yes,* I believe in God."

"You don't sound so sure."

"I'm sure," she said.

"Then why'd you have to think about it?"

"Because—" Rebecca said, chewing slowly. "It's complicated. For me, God is something specific. A symbol of good and hope. Something to aspire to. A role model, I guess."

"God is your *role model*? I thought your grandmother was your role model," I joked, remembering the essay we'd had to do for English homework last year. Mine was about Kalpana Chawla, who had been the first Indian American woman astronaut.

"Don't make fun of me; it's personal."

"I wasn't—promise. I was just thinking about that dumb English assignment—remember? When Ryan Berger said his role model was an RX-7?"

We used to laugh about that all the time, but now Rebecca seemed annoyed.

"You're changing the subject," she said.

I popped the last bite of PB&C into my mouth while I considered.

"Rebecca," I said thickly, "what if I don't believe in God?"

"Well, do you?"

"I don't know," I said. I really didn't. I wondered again if I *had to* in order to have a bat mitzvah.

I mean, what if I had to swear an oath before God and everyone that I believed in Him? I'd never heard of that happening at a bar mitzvah, but then again, I didn't know Hebrew too well. Maybe they slipped it in somewhere between the last *aliyah* and the *haftarah*. What if I was swearing and I didn't even know it? I could promise to *try*. I could promise to be a good person. But beyond that—I didn't know.

Chapter 15

At my bat mitzvah lesson on Monday, Rabbi Aron asked me if I had any ideas for my speech, which he called my "remarks." My Torah portion was the one about Joseph and his coat of many colors—except Rabbi told me it may or may not have had many colors and it may or may not have been a coat. More contradictions.

"I don't get it," I said. "Why can't it just be a coat? I mean—why does everything require interpretation? It's very . . ."

"Ambiguous?" Rabbi Aron offered.

"I was going to say *frustrating*, but yeah."

"Would you like it better if you were told exactly what to think?" he asked, a faint smile on his lips.

"No."

"Didn't think so. Without ambiguity, there could be no debate. Debate is a good thing, a useful thing. Have you heard of dialectics?"

"Not really," I said, not wanting to sound stupid.

"It's a philosophical method, a device, really—a way, through discussion and questioning of each other's ideas, to reach a satisfactory answer together."

I understood we were no longer talking about anything as trivial as Joseph's coat.

"You've read the *parashah*, I presume?" Rabbi asked.

I'd read it, and I didn't like it. I mean—Joseph was so full of himself, probably because Jacob spoiled him rotten even though he had, like, eleven other kids and two wives. In fact, don't even get me started on Jacob—in class the week before, we had just read how he cheated his brother Esau out of his birthright; yet, which one of them got to be our forefather? That's right. Jacob.

"Can you find a lesson in it, Tara?" Rabbi asked, predictably.

"Yeah," I said, recalling the conversation with Rebecca on Sunday. "Jacob was a terrible role model."

"Say again?"

"Think about it. Jacob cheated *his* elder brother out of his birthright. Now we're all supposed to look up to Jacob and not Esau. How is that right? And Joseph learned everything he knows from him. *That's* why his brothers sold him to the Ishmaelites as a slave. Speaking of which—" I said, thinking again of Rebecca's *parashah*. "Never mind."

I guess I sounded upset, because Rabbi folded his hands and said, "Is something wrong, Tara?"

I sighed. "You know Rebecca?"

Rabbi smiled. "Yes, of course."

"Well, then you know she got Mishpatim—Laws—and, well, I don't understand it."

"What don't you understand?"

"About the slaves."

"I know, right?" Rabbi said, sounding just like Rebecca. "Think about *that*."

"I am thinking about it. And what I think is—isn't that a little bit hypocritical?"

"Maybe a lot!" Rabbi agreed.

"To own slaves, I mean, when your entire religion is about being freed from slavery."

"I wouldn't say that's what the *entire* religion is about, Tara," Rabbi said. "But you ask a valid question." Not that he was going to tell me the answer, as I could see.

"I know." I sighed. "You're going to tell me to look it up."

"Actually, I was going to ask you to be patient and save your questions for later. We'll be discussing it in the spring. I expect your friend Rebecca will be something of an expert on the topic by then." Rabbi looked at his watch. "Before you go . . . I'd like to know: Do your parents know your grandmother liberated you from Hebrew school yesterday?"

I gulped. It was probably a sin to lie to a rabbi, so I didn't answer him.

"How did you know I was with Gran?" I asked. "Did Sheila Rosenberg snitch?"

"Sheila Rosenberg is many things, Tara Feinstein, but she is not a snitch. Your grandmother called me herself, yesterday afternoon."

"She did?"

"She did indeed," said Rabbi. "Her timing was fortu-itous. I was about to call your parents. Which is why I am asking you, do they know?"

I shook my head. "They don't, but they will soon, I promise. And I won't be absent again."

"Very well. And no more fighting, you understand?"

So he knew about that, too.

Chapter 16

ebecca's lesson was right after mine, so I sat on the steps to wait for her. My head was full of the topics Rabbi and I had just talked about. It was a lot to take in, and I had a sneaking suspicion he had been demonstrating that "dialectics" thing on me with all his questions.

In a way, it was a relief not being told exactly what to think. If everything was open to discussion, then just maybe there were no wrong answers. I mean, there's the Ten Commandments, obviously. I think we can all agree about those. Beyond that, there was room for debate. Just like in real life.

I still hadn't worked up the courage to ask Rabbi about believing in God. I didn't know if I ever would.

I started thinking about my speech. What was there to say about Joseph that hadn't already been said a million times? The gist was, Joseph was the second youngest of twelve brothers, the older of the two sons of Jacob's favorite wife, Rachel. Jacob loved him the best and gave him a special coat that made his brothers mad jealous. Then Joseph started having these dreams that meant his brothers were going to have to bow down to him, and he was conceited enough to tell them about it, so of course they hated him and plotted against him.

I took out my Hebrew school notebook and started doodling with a fine-point green Sharpie. I drew a stick-figure Joseph falling into a ditch, while his brothers all pointed and laughed. I don't have any brothers or sisters, but if I did, I could kind of understand how Joseph's had felt. I mean, he sort of had it coming. If you went around telling people your big-headed dreams about how you're destined to rule over them someday, you shouldn't be surprised when they rip your coat and tell people you're dead.

I could also see how they were wrong—how they were too quick to get mad, instead of seeing the possibilities. I mean, if your brother was going to be the king or whatever, didn't that have some advantages? "We make our own opportunities"—Gran always said that. Meaning, change could be good, if you seize the day or whatever. Sometimes.

I wondered if I could do something with the many-colored coat and my many-colored sari. I mean, there had to be some symbolism in that. I sucked on the pen cap, pondering where I could go with it.

Recently, my auntie gave me a beautiful sari that once belonged to my great-grandmother. Like my sari, Joseph's coat (which, by the way, maybe wasn't a coat) had many colors . . . or then again, maybe it didn't.

I drew a big savage green X through the paragraph and went back to doodling in the margin: big, loopy vines and flowers and paisleys and stuff, like *mehndi*—those henna tattoos people do for Indian weddings or just for fun. When I ran out of room in the margin, I switched to doodling on the palm of my left hand and up the inside of my arm.

"What are you doing?"

I looked up to see Sheila Rosenberg standing on the bottom step. I sighed and closed my notebook.

"Nothing," I said. "Thinking about my *parashah*."

"Which one did you get?"

"Vayeishev," I said. "It's the one about—"

"—Joseph," she said. "Mine's Bereishit." *In the Beginning.*

"That's a hard one," I said, thinking, *Mostly because you have to say "Bereishit" with a straight face.*

Sheila nodded. "Rabbi says it's the most important one. Because it's first."

She kept talking, but I wasn't really listening. Sometimes I couldn't help staring at her. She had enormous, curly black hair, pale blue eyes, and paler bluish skin that Mum said looked like porcelain and Rebecca said looked like skim milk. She was pretty, kind of, in the way dolls are pretty. And dolls gave me the creeps.

Sheila was still talking about our *parashahs* when I tuned back in. "Kind of ironic," she was saying. "You getting the one about clothes." *So rude.*

"That's not really what it's about, you know."

"I know," she said, awkwardly. "I was just kidding."

I stared her down. I *really* wanted to shove her again. Down the steps this time.

"So," she said, twisting a strand of hair around her finger, "what do you think?"

"About what?"

"What I just asked you," she said. Her cheeks went bright red, and she stared at her feet.

I had no idea what she was talking about. Also, I still had a tingling in my arm from wanting to push her down the stairs, and I was afraid if she didn't move away IMMEDIATELY, I might accidentally do it. Probably she only wanted me to admit that Bereishit was the most important *parashah* or something equally petty. If it would make her go away . . .

"Fine," I said.

She smiled. "Yay!" she said, making little cheerleader motions with her hands.

Whatever. I didn't really care.

When we saw Rebecca coming out, Sheila looked at her watch. Her lesson was next. "Gotta go!" she said.

I saw them stop and chat amiably in the vestibule, and I couldn't help noticing they seemed kind of chummy all of a sudden. *What's that all about?* I wondered. But then Sheila went in and Rebecca came out, and we got to talking about something else entirely, and I forgot all about it.

ran was playing a round of solitaire when I got home from my bat mitzvah lesson.

"How come you don't play on the computer like everyone else?" I asked.

"Because you can't cheat at computer solitaire."

"You *cheat*?" I squealed.

"Keep your voice down. It's not cheating if it's solitaire." She gathered up the cards in a neat stack. That was when she noticed my arm doodles. "What's this *shmutz* all over you?" She licked her thumb and started scrubbing my arm, hard.

"Eww, Gran, quit it! That's how you spread germs."

"What germs? I'm your grandmother."

"It's not *shmutz*," I said. "It's supposed to be a tattoo."

"A tattoo?" Gran shrieked. "I'll murder you."

"Not a real tattoo. A temporary one. *Mehndi*."

"Mendy who?"

"*Mehndi* is a what, not a who. Henna tattoo. Except I used a pen."

"Go scrub that off."

"I would, Gran, except . . . it was kind of a permanent marker."

"*Meshugge* kid," Gran muttered. She stood up. "Ready to get down to business?"

"Ready as I'm gonna be," I said, sounding braver than I felt. "Let's do this."

We knocked on Mum's office door.

"It's open," she called.

I shuffled in behind Gran.

"Now, Rita, don't have a meltdown," Gran said, right to the point. Which was not an auspicious start. Mum looked up in a panic. I handed her the ruined sari and sat down meekly in one of the chairs opposite her desk.

"My God, Tara," she said when she saw the damage.

"Take it easy, Rita," Gran said. "We have a plan."

"We," Mum echoed.

She sat absolutely still as Gran explained everything. When it came time to describe the dress, Gran draped the fabric over me as if I was a human mannequin. Mum nodded slowly.

"Marvin is capable?" she asked reasonably.

"Absolutely!" Gran said.

"He's already in on this, then?" Mum shot me a look. I stared at the floor.

"Why not?" Gran said. "We're coming to you with a solution instead of a problem."

"We," Mum repeated.

"The child was terrified," Gran said. *Terrified?* Okay, maybe a little. She pinched the back of my arm. "She came to me for help. We didn't *do* anything before talking to you."

Mum unpinned the old photo from the wall—the one of her and Meena at their aunt's wedding—and stared at it grimly, her lips pressed thin. She sighed.

"Do you know, I was never allowed to wear that sari as a child? Meena was the older, responsible one. How I begged Mumma to let me wear it."

"I never knew that, Mum."

"Of course you didn't. How would you?"

"I'm really sorry," I whispered. I felt my chin wobble. Mum seemed to make up her mind.

"It is a lovely piece of fabric," she admitted. "And I always would have preferred you in a dress."

"It's settled, then!" Gran cried, clapping her hands. "I'll call Marvin."

"No," Mum said, sitting up straight. "You've done quite enough. *I'll* call Marvin."

"Suit yourself," Gran said. "Tell him I'll call him later."

"Of course you will," Mum said darkly. "You two, out now. Shoo."

"Gran," I said, flinging myself at her after we closed the door behind us, "you're my hero."

"Get off me," Gran said. "I just had my hair done."

"When?" I teased.

Gran shook her fist at me. "You're a rotten, ungrateful kid."

"So I've been told," I said, hugging her even tighter.

Chapter 18

In Social Studies on Wednesday, Jake Solomon brought in an article about the Middle East, and he kept referring to the Palestinians as Pakistanis, as if they were all the same.

"Pakistan isn't even in the Middle East," I said. "It's right next to India. That's like mixing up Israelis and Icelanders."

For some reason, that sparked a heated debate, even though I was only pointing out geography. People can be oversensitive. And Ms. Ross lost control of the discussion, of course.

At lunchtime, the whole seventh grade was still obsessing over it, even kids who weren't in Ross's class.

I was just minding my own business, eating lunch with Ben-o and Rebecca at our usual table. Sheila Rosenberg was next to Rebecca, her nose buried in a book. Aisha Khan was down at the other end of the table with Jenna Alberts.

At the next table, Ryan Berger was imitating Ross's high-pitched, nasal voice, which made everyone laugh. Then he got up for a second helping of lentil chili and the table quieted down.

A minute later, he was standing behind me.

"Settle a bet," he said. "Are Indians Muslim?"

"What?" I turned to give him a quizzical look.

I was getting that uneasy feeling like a fight was about to happen. I didn't want to go blank and start swinging. Not with Ryan asking such a stupid question and everyone at both tables watching, suddenly quiet again. Why was he singling me out? I wasn't even the only Indian in the lunchroom. I mean, why didn't he ask Aisha, who *does* happen to be both Indian and Muslim? Asking if Indians are Muslims was like asking if Americans are Jews—some are, and some aren't. It depends.

"Some are, yes," I said slowly. "Some aren't."

"Are you?"

"Am I what?"

"A Muslim. Duh."

"I'm in your *Hebrew school*," I reminded him. I felt defensive, backed into a position of denying being Muslim, as if it were somehow the wrong thing to be. Aisha was watching, waiting to hear how I would answer. Even Sheila Rosenberg looked up from the book she was reading to give Ryan a withering look.

"You know full well she's a practicing Jew," she said.

"Why's she still practicing—doesn't she get it yet?" Ryan asked, cracking himself up so hard, I was afraid the plate of chili was going to slide off his tray and onto my head.

But he did have a point—something about the way Sheila said "practicing" made it sound like I wasn't a real Jew, just acting like one, maybe even hiding a secret Muslim identity.

"Would you *please* move, Ryan?" I said. "You're making me nervous back there."

"What? You scared of everyone finding out you're a terrorist?"

"If anyone is terrorizing people, it's you," I yelled.

And then he said it, the horrible thing: "My grandpa says all Muslims are terrorists."

Just maybe he was kidding, being sarcastic, mocking people who thought that way. But it wasn't funny. And those soulless eyes of his weren't giving anything away. I glanced toward Aisha. She and Jenna had stopped talking and had turned around to listen.

"A, I'm not a Muslim. B, you're a racist."

"It's not racist if it's true."

Gran once taught me a handy trick that I use all the time. She said to take any remark that you suspect might be racist and substitute the word *Jew*. If you're insulted by it, it's probably racist. I wouldn't stand for anyone saying all Jews were terrorists, or all Indians for that matter, so I stood up and let Ryan Berger have it, accidentally-on-purpose knocking the tray back into his stupid face. I honestly didn't mean to hurt him physically, just knock the lentil chili off his plate and onto him and his clothes.

Ryan yelped and put his hands up to his face. The tray clattered to the floor in a gloopy mess. Lentils were oozing down the front of his shirt. Ben-o handed him a well-used napkin, which broke the mood. Jenna Alberts laughed. But blood was beginning to trickle from Ryan's nose. I panicked.

"Fight! Fight!" some sixth-graders chanted. Sully, the ex-Marine-turned-lunchroom-supervisor, came barreling toward us and grabbed Ryan by the collar.

"She hit me!" Ryan told Sullivan, removing one hand from his face to point an accusing finger at me. And then, you wouldn't believe it, but Sheila Rosenberg came to my defense. She even lied a little bit.

"She didn't hit him, Mr. Sullivan. He was standing behind her when she stood up. She knocked his tray by accident. She didn't push him or anything," she added, giving me a pointed look.

"What'd I tell you about fighting with girls, Berger?" Sully bawled, frog-marching Ryan to the nurse's office.

When they were gone, I straightened my shirt and sat down, glaring around the table.

"Still think Berger has a 'thing' for me?" I spat, rounding on Ben-o.

"Sure, why not?" he said. "Couples fight all the time. Just look at my parents."

Disgusted, I ignored him and turned on Sheila. "And *you*—who asked you to get involved?"

She shrugged. "He's been asking for it," she said, wiping a lump of lentil chili off her math book.

I should have left it alone, but I was still pumped up.

"Why did you say that about me being a *practicing* Jew? Like I'm not completely Jewish?"

"That's not what it means."

"Why didn't you just say 'she's Jewish'?" Sheila didn't answer. "It's because of my mother, isn't it? How many times do I have to tell you, she's Jewish."

"I know," Sheila said. "You're being a little paranoid."

Maybe I was. I stomped over to an empty table to cool off.

Aisha touched my arm. "Are you okay?"

"Yeah," I said. "Just catching my breath."

"You really shouldn't get into so many fights. You're going to get in trouble someday."

"But you heard him—"

"He said his *grandfather*," Aisha cut in hastily. "He can't help that. *My* grandparents have some pretty outrageous things to say about Jews. Nothing I can do about that, except ignore it."

I looked down at my hands, wondering if I'd ever learn to ignore things, or if I even wanted to.

"Look," Aisha went on, "Ryan's just a doofus. I'm pretty sure he thought he was being ironic. He doesn't even know when he's being offensive." She laughed. "But I think he knows it now, thanks to you."

＊＊＊

I was surprised when Ryan showed up for Robotics Club later that afternoon, still smelling faintly like chili.

"It's not broken," he said.

"What?"

"My nose." I wouldn't look at him, so he stuck his face close to mine and said, "Wanna try again?"

I almost smiled, but then I remembered what he said that had set me off. "You shouldn't say stuff like you said at lunch," I said. "You shouldn't even think it."

"I know," Ryan said, getting out of my face. "I didn't even mean it. I was just mocking Ross, at first. It was mean and stupid."

"You should tell that to Aisha, not me."

"I already did."

"You did?"

"Yep."

"What did she say?"

Ryan shrugged. "We're besties again."

"You were never besties."

"I know—listen," he said, scratching his head, "somebody said something dumb about Adam. I got mad. I shouldn't have taken it out on you or anyone else."

"Who? What did they say?"

Ryan shook his head. "I'm not going to repeat it."

I glanced over at Adam and Ben-o on the opposite side of the room. Whatever it was, Adam didn't seem overly affected by it. He and Ben-o were having an animated discussion about their robot.

"Adam's like me," I said. "He doesn't look like who he is. But that doesn't make him any less . . . himself."

"I know," said Ryan. "That's why I got mad. And the school shrink says I lash out inappropriately when I get mad."

"Like the Hulk?"

"No—like ADHD."

"That explains a lot, actually," I said.

Ryan laughed.

"I'm sorry I gave you a bloody nose," I said.

Ryan shrugged. "Got me out of math class. I owe you one."

"Did the nurse call your mom?"

"Yeah, but I told her it was a regular nosebleed. I used to get them all the time. I can't have anyone know a girl beat me up. Even a girl as tough as Tara Feinstein."

I smiled at the compliment. Still smiling, I went to the cabinet for supplies. Ben-o came up behind me.

"Hey."

"Hey."

"See any nine-volt batteries in there?"

"Bottom shelf," I said.

Ryan came up and tapped me on the shoulder.

"Need me to draw anything?" he asked. I saw Ben-o's back stiffen.

"No," I said. "I thought we could start working on a prototype."

"A what?"

"Like—test out the design."

"Oh," Ryan said, looking kind of lost. I felt a little sorry for him.

"Maybe you can make a ramp," I said. "Out of a piece of cardboard."

"I can do that!" Ryan said, heading for the pile of flattened cardboard boxes near the door.

"Made up already?" Ben-o asked, clearly annoyed. "That was fast."

"Let it go, Ben-o—please." I sighed. "I'm having a crappy day, if you didn't notice." He bent down to get the batteries, then stalked away. I'd forgotten what I went to the closet for, so I just grabbed a bunch of markers and went back to my table.

I looked over, but he and Adam had the spy shield up again, so I couldn't see what they were doing. Deshaun and Marina were poring over an old issue of *ROBO* magazine. Mr. H had a couple of the sixth-graders testing batteries. Max and Joe were tinkering with a motorized wheel set.

Ryan worked on the ramp for all of ten minutes before he lost interest, and then he left early—he said he wanted to run home and change his shirt before his mom got home and smelled the chili on him. That left me to clean up after him again.

After Robotics, I waited for Ben-o at the door while he said good-bye to Adam. Then we walked home together—alone for the first time in like forever. He didn't tease me about Ryan again.

"Hey—are you coming over Saturday?" I asked.

"Of course," Ben-o said.

"It's my turn to pick, you know."

"I know," he said, groaning.

"Don't be like that. We can watch any movie you want. I don't mind."

Ben-o grinned and I knew we were okay for now. We hadn't talked much since the basketball incident in the park two weeks before. We'd even missed movie night again on Saturday—this time because he was visiting his grandmother in Queens. That was twice in a row.

"Anything?" he said, rubbing his hands together with evil glee. "Bwa-ha-ha-ha!"

"And one Bollywood."

"Aha! I knew it!"

I laughed and ran ahead, hoping he would run after me. That time in the park, when he left me there with Ryan and Adam, I had run after him. I couldn't catch him, but I had *tried*. I wanted him to do the same now, but he didn't. So I stopped and waited for him to catch up, feeling a little bit foolish, and resentful.

Chapter 19

On Saturday afternoon, I ran into Ben-o downstairs after I picked up the mail.

I almost didn't see him come in. There had been a letter for me in our mailbox. Actually, a bat mitzvah invitation. In a big, sparkly purple envelope that could only have come from one person: Sheila Rosenberg.

I hadn't expected to be invited, but maybe her parents were making her invite everyone, just like Ryan Berger's mom. Tucked inside the card was a note:

I'M SORRY I ONCE SAID YOU'RE NOT JEWISH.
YOU SHOULDN'T SHOVE PEOPLE, THOUGH.

That was big of her, especially after what happened at lunch on Wednesday—though she had probably mailed it before then.

"What's that?" Ben-o asked, coming up behind me.

I turned around, then did a double take, almost laughing

in his face. Almost, but not quite. It took just about all of my self-control.

"A bat mitzvah invitation," I squeaked, getting my face under control. "Nice haircut."

"Thanks," he said, kicking the floor a little. "I took your advice."

"What do you mean, my advice?"

"Remember when you said to let it be natural or shave it all off? Well. There you go."

"I liked it curly," I said. I'd never noticed before, but Ben-o had enormous ears, like a sippy cup.

A little while later, when he came over for movie night, Mum answered the door.

"Don't you look handsome, Benjamin!" she said. I smirked. Ben-o's ears turned an alarming shade of red.

"I say, old chap," Daddy said, slapping Ben-o on the back. "Joining the navy?"

Mum pulled him into the kitchen.

We stood there awkwardly for a few moments. I couldn't stop staring at his head, trying to picture him the way he'd looked the day before, and every day his whole life.

"You don't like it," he said.

"No, I do! I *said* nice haircut."

Ben-o scratched his head.

To change the subject, I asked him if he wanted to go see the new asteroids exhibit at the Museum of Natural History on Sunday, but he said he'd already seen it. With Jenna.

"Jenna Alberts?" I didn't even know they were friends. I mean, sure, we all eat lunch together, but, like—friend-friends. One time last spring, I overheard her telling Aisha that Ben-o was one of the cutest boys in our grade. I wondered if it was mutual. Was that what Ben-o had been up to the last two weeks? Was she his girlfriend? As his best friend, where did that leave me?

"It's just that you've been so busy lately," Ben-o said, reading my mind. "With Hebrew school and all." Which was *true*, but it still sounded like an excuse.

Anyway, there he was, with his ridiculous ears sticking out, somehow looking adorable—vulnerable and shy and unable to hide what he was thinking or feeling. It occurred to me to ask him point-blank about Jenna and see what his ears had to say about it.

I bit my lip. "How does she like your new 'do?"

"Who?"

"Jenna."

Ben-o's ears promptly turned red again. "I haven't seen her yet."

"Oh," I said. Had he really cut his hair off for me, because I'd said so? That was crazy. I wouldn't chop off my hair for anyone. Not even Ben-o. But I couldn't let it go. "Are you worried what she'll think?"

"No. Why would I be?"

"Well, she'll probably like it."

"Why do you keep talking about Jenna?" he asked, seeming puzzled by my questions. Was he actually clueless, or just pretending? Maybe he wasn't into her after all. Maybe they were just friends. For whatever reason, though, that didn't make me feel any better. "Besides," he said, "she knew I was going to do it."

"She did?"

"Yeah," he said, rubbing his stubbly head. "She told me not to. But I said it's only hair—it grows back."

I tried to picture Ben-o and Jenna Alberts having a serious conversation about haircuts. It seemed so weird and—intimate. So like best friends. And then I knew why I was jealous.

"What?" he said when he saw my expression.

"Nothing," I said, shaking it off with effort. "Ready to watch a DVD?"

"Sure," he said, grinning. He held up his binder.

"Mine first," I sang. "House rules."

Ben-o got settled on the couch.

"What are we watching, anyway?"

"You'll see," I said, popping in the DVD.

"Oh, no." He groaned as the Indian music started up. "Not this one again."

"You haven't seen this one."

"They're all the same."

I suppressed a giggle. Half the fun of watching Bollywood movies with Ben-o is seeing him squirm through the sentimental goop. Even so, I fast-forwarded through the embarrassing love scenes and the most high-pitched songs, so it was over in like forty minutes.

"Want to watch yours now?" I asked as soon as it ended.

"Not yet," Ben-o said.

"Okay. Want to play Stingray?" I asked, remembering how, before, we'd found it easier to talk to each other while we were playing. That was the time we had watched *Bloody Fools* and Ben-o had put his arm around me. I hadn't given it a second thought at the time, but—with what I knew now—had he been trying something? Would he try again? I didn't know if I wanted him to or not.

I mean, this was Ben-o and me. Best friends since forever. For no reason at all, I thought about what it would be like to kiss him. I wondered what his mouth would taste like. The thought was so embarrassing, I felt my skin grow hot.

"Not right now," Ben-o said. "Listen—I wanted to tell you . . . I made the regionals in chess again this year."

"That's awesome!" I cried, grateful for a neutral topic. "Congratulations."

"I know you don't like chess and all—"

"I don't not like chess," I said.

"Okay—well, I was wondering if you want to come with my dad and me? Mom has to stay home with Nina. I know it's kind of boring—"

"Yes," I said, jumping at the offer.

"Yes, it's boring?"

"Yes, I'll go with you. When is it?"

"It's on the second Saturday in October, on Long Island somewhere. My dad's driving."

"Uh-oh . . ."

"I know." Ben-o laughed. His dad grew up right here in Manhattan, so he never learned to drive more than about twenty miles an hour. "So, you'll come?"

"I said I would."

"Sure you don't have to go to any bar mitzvahs that day?"

"Not that I know of," I said. "I have this really cool date-book, you know. I'll write it down in there."

"Cool," Ben-o said. He looked so happy, I realized how long it had been since he'd smiled at me like that.

"Want to watch your movie now?"

"Sure," said Ben-o. "It's a full moon tonight, so I thought . . ."

"Let me guess." I laughed. "*Where, Oh, Werewolf*?"

"Exactly," said Ben-o.

We watched the movie, and he didn't try anything. In a way, it was a relief. Maybe it had been my imagination after all.

After the movie, we played a couple levels of Stingray.

"How's your bar mitzvah thing going?" Ben-o asked.

"*Bat* mitzvah," I corrected him, feeling a little bit like Sheila Rosenberg. "Boys have bar mitzvahs."

"Right," said Ben-o. "Is it—are you—all good now?"

"What do you mean, 'all good'?"

"Like, you're doing it, right?"

"Yeah," I said. "Turns out I didn't have a choice after all. Not that I'm against it."

"Now you sound like me." Ben-o laughed.

"I didn't mean to sound—flippant," I said, pulling out one of Mum's favorite fifty-cent words. "I decided I really want to go through with it. Even though I still have questions. Rabbi says I ask more questions than anyone he's ever known. But I like it. It's kind of interesting. I'm finding out things."

"What kind of things?"

"Like . . ." I thought about telling him what I'd learned about Joseph and his brothers, or the bit about slavery, or the whole dialectics thing that Rabbi had tried to explain to me, but it was kind of a jumble in my head, too complicated for a quick summary. "Lots of things! I'm still kind of sorting it out," I said. "But it's all good. I think."

"That's cool," Ben-o said. "I think."

✳ ✳ ✳

After he left, I took out my datebook and flipped to the second Saturday in October. I wrote BEN-O'S CHESS TOURNAMENT in big block letters. Something was nagging at me. I went to the hall table, where I had dropped the mail earlier, and fished out the big purple invitation. Sheila's bat mitzvah. It was the same day.

Sorry, Sheila, I thought. *But not that sorry.*

Chapter 20

Rebecca came over after Hebrew school the next morning. She had been up in Stamford all day Saturday for her cousin Jonah's bar mitzvah, so we had a lot of catching up to do.

Rebecca was full of new information. Apparently Jonah had had something called a "cultural" bar mitzvah, which was a new one to me—he hadn't had to read from the Torah or do a *haftarah* or anything, just research a secular Jewish topic and give a speech on it. Rebecca's dad told her that most kids who have a "cultural" bar mitzvah do it on principle—like, because they're atheists or agnostics, or their parents are progressives, but they still want to be socially Jewish.

"Jonah did that?" I asked, skeptical. I remembered Rebecca's cousin as a whiny asthmatic with a runny nose and a short attention span. Not a deep thinker.

Rebecca laughed. "Aunt Meredith isn't exactly progressive. And Jonah isn't smart enough to have thought of it himself. My guess is he forgot to study and ran out of time.

Anyway, I was thinking—maybe *you* should have a cultural bat mitzvah."

"Why?"

"I don't mean anything negative. Just, since you're not sure."

"I already know my *haftarah* practically by heart," I said defensively.

"Okay. It was just an idea. I thought it was interesting. Any news on the, um . . . ?" she asked, glancing furtively toward Mum's office.

I shook my head. "Marvin's still working on it."

"I'm really sorry," Rebecca whispered for like the hundredth time.

"It's not your fault," I said, for like the hundred and first.

"Well, if I can do something, maybe help you pay for it with my allowance . . ."

That was sweet of her, but silly. I smiled and shook my head.

"Gran is taking care of it," I said. To make her feel better, I put on my best Meena Auntie imitation. "It was belonging to Daadiji. It was the one good thing she was bringing from Lahore to Delhi during the Partition."

Rebecca didn't laugh. "Wow," she said. "I don't even know what that means, but it sounds important."

I wasn't surprised she didn't know about Partition; most American kids didn't. Mum once explained it to me this way: Try to imagine the place where you were born being split into two different countries, separated by majority language, ethnicity, and religion. And suddenly, in the house you grew up in, in the city where you were born, you were an outcast—a minority. That's pretty much what happened to a lot of people in India and Pakistan during Partition, in 1947. Millions of people fled in both directions—Hindus and Sikhs to India, Muslims to Pakistan. Sometimes with nothing more than what they could carry. Mum's grandparents, my great-grandparents, left Lahore, in what was now Pakistan, in the middle of the night. My great-grandmother put every piece of jewelry she had in the sari and tied it up around her waist, under her traveling clothes. Nanaji was three years old. His baby sister died before they reached the refugee camp in Delhi. My great-grandmother sold off all the jewelry for food. The only good thing she kept was the gold-threaded sari.

It had survived Partition, and now I had ruined it.

"Are you going to be in a lot of trouble?" Rebecca asked. "I mean, if your uncle can't . . ."

"Cousin," I said. "But it's still not your fault." I didn't want to talk about it anymore.

"So . . . what did you do last night? Oh, right—your weekly movie date with your boyfriend."

"What's that supposed to mean?"

"What it sounds like," Rebecca said.

"Don't be stupid," I said. "Benjamin and I have been best friends forever."

"I thought *I* was your best friend forever. And excuse me—*um*, 'Benjamin'?"

"It just came out that way," I said, blushing.

"How adorable."

"Shut up. You're my best friend, too," I said. "It's different with Ben-o. We're practically like brother and sister."

"*That's* gross," Rebecca said. "So what did you and, um, *Benjamin* do on this not-date?"

What was Rebecca getting at? I mean, I'd had my suspicions lately, but I hadn't told her about them. Or that I'd accidentally fantasized about kissing him. Or any of the hundred weird ways Ben-o had been acting lately.

"Watched DVDs," I said. "As usual."

"Chick flick or dude movie?"

"One of each. A musical and a stupid horror movie."

"Aw," Rebecca said. "Did he hold your hand during the scary parts?"

"What planet are you on?"

"Who made the first move?" she persisted. "Were you the kisser or the kissee?" Rebecca started making smoochy sounds, so I jammed a pillow in her face. That settled her down finally.

"Nobody kissed anybody," I said. "What is with you?"

She was in high gear. None of this felt like, "Oh, by the way . . ." It was as if she'd rehearsed it and then waited for any excuse to bring it up.

She pursed her lips. "He likes you, you know. I mean, really likes you."

"How do you know?"

"You know it, too," she insisted. "It's weird the way you don't admit it. You're giving him mixed signals."

"No, I'm not!"

"You are. Remember that time he tried to put his arm around you, maybe kiss you?"

"No."

"Yes, you do. One of your famous movie nights."

"Again—how do you know about that?"

Rebecca ignored me. "He thought you kind of felt the same way. But when he put his arm around you, you laughed at him."

"Not *at* him!" I cried. "Okay, maybe I giggled, but that's because I was nervous and because my dad was there. That's *all*. Besides, I thought he was kidding."

"He's worried about you and Berger."

"Shut. Up!" I yelled. "I'm so sick of Ryan Berger this and Ryan Berger that."

Rebecca looked impatient. "The point is, whether you can see it or not, Ryan has a crush on you, too."

"You don't know that."

"I do know it. Want to know how?" She didn't wait for me to answer. "Because Ryan told Adam, and Adam told Ben-o, that you're the hottest girl in our Hebrew school. I'm third, by the way. After Missy Abrams."

I laughed at that, a little cruelly. "Tell Ben-o not to worry," I said. "I am not interested in Berger."

"Ben-o was there when Sheila said Ryan's only allowed to date Jewish people, remember? So now Ben-o thinks maybe you're only interested in Jewish boys."

"That's totally racist!"

"No," Rebecca said. "He was just asking. Identifying with your culture is not the same thing as racism."

My culture? I thought. *Which one?*

"Anyway, how do you know all this?"

"Because Ben-o talks to me."

"He does?"

"Because I'm your *best friend*. And I'm Jewish. He wanted to know if that was the reason you were blowing him off."

"I'm not blowing him off! What did you tell him?"

"I told him to ask *you*. I take it he didn't. You two are exactly alike—you think you have this weird telepathic communication thing going on, but you don't. Just because you both say things in your head doesn't mean you can *hear* each other."

"Rebecca—" I bit my lip. "When you start dating, are you only going to date Jewish people?"

She thought for a moment. "I don't know. But I'm going to marry one, probably."

"How do you know that?"

Rebecca shrugged. "I just do," she said.

That blew my mind. I mean, I didn't know if I'd ever get married, but if I did, it would be in like thirty years, like two and a half lifetimes from now. I was worried about my bat mitzvah and the Robotics finals in the spring. Why were we talking about marriage?

I looked at her hard, trying to figure out where this was coming from. "You're starting to sound like Sheila Rosenberg. Have you been hanging out with her or something? Oh, right, I forgot. She's your math tutor."

"Back to the main subject," Rebecca said. "You have no respect for Ben-o's feelings."

"But I like things the way they are."

"That's a little selfish, don't you think?"

"Why?"

"Never mind—best friend, boyfriend, it's up to you. Just don't keep calling him your brother, okay? Because you're breaking his heart. *Now*"—she threw open her Hebrew book—"are we studying? Because if not, I have to go home. I have an *enormous* math test next week. I should really be studying with Sheila."

"Are you mad at me for something I did to Ben-o?"

"Me? I don't care what you do. He's *your* friend."

"Whoa! I'm confused. Weren't you just standing up for him?"

"I have nothing against Ben-o, you dope. It's that— you've been stuck in your own little world lately, you know? Did you seriously not know he likes you?"

"I seriously did not know," I swore. It was only a partial lie. I wondered what else I'd been missing lately.

We studied in silence for a while, and then Rebecca said she had to go.

"Oh—one more thing, Tara," she said as she was leaving. "You might want to take a look in your datebook. At Valentine's Day, to be exact. In case you still don't believe me."

After she left, I got out the datebook and flipped to February fourteenth. There was a heart drawn in red pencil around the number fourteen. That was it. I got the message.

Chapter 21

’d pretty much forgotten about Sheila's invitation until Rebecca reminded me about it on Monday.

"I forgot to ask you yesterday when we were . . . you know," she said. "You're going, right?"

"Can't," I said. "That's Ben-o's chess tournament."

"You don't even like chess."

"I don't not like chess," I said.

"But you have to come. You promised."

"Who?"

"Sheila."

"I didn't promise her anything. I didn't even know I was invited."

"I asked Sheila to invite you. And you said yes."

"I have no idea what you're talking about."

"That time? After your bat mitzvah lesson? Sheila told me you said yes."

Was that what Sheila had asked me when I wasn't listening? How did Rebecca even know that? I flashed back to their conversation in the vestibule. I hadn't been able to hear them through the glass doors, of course, but even then I'd noticed they had seemed kind of chummy. And they *had* been sitting next to each other at lunch, but I thought that was only because Sheila was tutoring Rebecca in math.

I *did* say yes. Only I'd had no idea what I was saying yes to. "I thought we were talking about Bereishit," I mused. Out loud, apparently.

"What?"

"Nothing. Listen—I promised Ben-o, too, and he's more important. You said so yourself."

"More important than me?"

"This has nothing to do with you."

"It has everything to do with me," she said, stamping her foot. "Wake up, Tara. I asked her to invite you, and you told her yes. Is it so wrong for me to want my two best friends to get along?"

"Hold up! You're best friends with Sheila ROSENBERG?"

"You know another Sheila?" Rebecca sighed.

"Since when . . . ?"

"You know, you're doing that thing again," Rebecca said. "Whenever you don't like someone, you always call them by their first and last name."

"You're changing the subject."

"Promise me you'll go," Rebecca said.

"I can't promise," I said. "It depends on Ben-o."

I was trapped—having to decide which of my two best friends to betray by choosing between two events I wasn't even a little bit interested in going to. Despite my protest to the contrary, I knew the chess tournament would be deadly boring to watch, and Sheila's bat mitzvah wasn't my idea of a good time either.

"Fine," said Rebecca, but I could tell it wasn't.

"You're the one who said I'm giving him mixed signals, remember?" I fumed. "When was that? Oh, right—yesterday! Or was that before you decided Sheila Rosenberg was your new best friend?"

"I didn't DECIDE," Rebecca yelled. "It happened. And it wasn't yesterday. It's been MONTHS. You'd know that if you ever paid attention to anyone but yourself."

Ouch. Maybe I was in my own little world—which was about to get even littler. So, what now? Was I supposed to walk up to Ben-o and say, "Hey, I know we're best friends and all, and Rebecca confirmed you have a crush on me, and I know I promised to go to your boring chess tournament, but I have to go to SHEILA ROSENBERG's stupid bat mitzvah instead, because I promised my *other* best friend I would be nice to *her* other best friend who I didn't even know existed"? *Yeah, that'd work.*

✳ ✳ ✳

After homeroom, I waited for Ben-o near his locker.

"It's okay," he said when I broke the news to him—about

Sheila's bat mitzvah, not the other stuff. He shrugged. "You've got your priorities."

I wanted to tell him, *You're my priority*, but I felt too timid all of a sudden, plus that wouldn't explain why I was going to Sheila's bat mitzvah instead of his chess tournament.

"Is Ryan going?" he asked.

"No, Rebecca says he's not invited. Why?" I asked, knowing full well why.

"No reason," he said. "He just keeps turning up. Like a bad penny."

"Ben-o . . ." I said, weary beyond words. "Ryan Berger and I are like sworn enemies."

"You mean that thing in the lunchroom? Looked like a lovers' quarrel to me."

"Don't be disgusting."

"I just thought—you know—with your bat mitzvah and all."

"What?" I wanted to make him say it.

"That you might be looking for someone—you know."

"You're an idiot," I said.

"Why is that so idiotic? Adam said—"

"Adam's *Korean*."

"No, he's not. He's adopted."

"I know!" I snapped. I felt bad for having said it. But I couldn't unsay it.

"It's cool," he said. "I'd totally understand."

"Well, there's nothing to understand. And, Ben-o—I'm really sorry about your chess tourney."

"It's okay." He shrugged. "I have someone else in mind."

Like, a backup?

"Who, Adam?"

"No, Jenna."

"Oh," I said, taken aback. "That's cool."

Of course it wasn't cool at all.

"You don't even like chess," he said for like the hundredth time.

Did Jenna like chess? I had no idea. More to the point, did Ben-o like Jenna more than me? Maybe Rebecca was right—maybe I hadn't been paying enough attention to my friends. I hadn't noticed that Rebecca was becoming BEST FRIENDS with Sheila Rosenberg or that Ben-o had been interested in me as more than a friend. For like ten minutes.

"For the hundredth time, I don't not like chess," I said lamely.

"Jenna's dad's been teaching her. She's really good! We've been practicing together. We're hoping she places in the next tournament so we can go to state together next year."

"We?" I echoed, feeling just like Mum must have felt when Gran and I came to her about the sari—left out. "It's cool," I said again. But it wasn't, really. I had finally gotten the message, but Ben-o had already moved on. To Jenna Alberts.

The bell rang, and we headed to our classes, in opposite directions.

* * *

"Ben-o and I had a fight," I accused Rebecca in English class. "I hope you're happy."

"Of course I'm not happy."

"He's taking Jenna Alberts to his chess tournament."

Rebecca's face fell. "Jenna really is into chess, you know."

"So I heard," I spat.

"Don't take this out on me," Rebecca said. "Or Jenna."

Jenna. The girl who thought Ben-o was one of the cutest boys in the seventh grade.

"I guess he's not into me after all," I said. All at once I saw it—how I was the go-to for hanging out and watching horror movies and eating ice cream and playing Stingray Rampage, while Jenna Alberts, with her golden skin, shiny hair, and hazel eyes, was girlfriend material. It should have been a relief.

"You're an idiot," Rebecca said, reading my mind.

The second bell rang, and I went back to my seat.

* * *

After school, I read Sheila's invitation again. The response card was the blank kind that didn't let you just say yes or no. I thought for a moment before I wrote:

Ms. Tara Feinstein would be delighted to attend.
P.S.

I was going to write *I forgive you for biting me,* but then I pictured Mrs. Rosenberg reading that. I was stuck with the P.S., though, so I wrote, as a kind of apology:

I know what you meant by "practicing."

That sounded stupid, so I crossed it out and wrote:

Thanks for inviting me.

I hoped I was making the right choice.

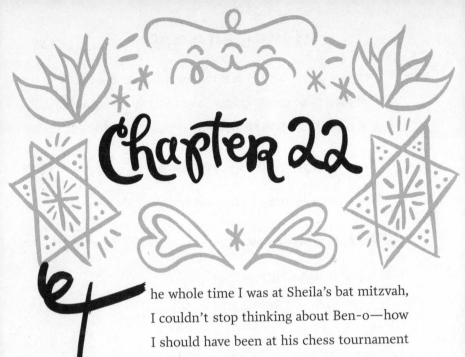

Chapter 22

The whole time I was at Sheila's bat mitzvah, I couldn't stop thinking about Ben-o—how I should have been at his chess tournament instead of sitting in temple wearing an itchy wool dress. Mum and I had finally agreed on a light gray dress with little pearl buttons down the front. I wanted to cut off the pearls and replace them with something funkier, like big neon pink safety pins or giant peace sign buttons, but Mum said she would absolutely skin me alive if I made any modifications to it whatsoever. She did make me wear one of her big colorful scarves, though, so I wouldn't look like I was dressed for a funeral instead of a bat mitzvah. And I persuaded her to let me wear neon pink tights, so it was an okay compromise.

Sheila made a decent speech about remaining true to yourself, your family, and your friends, and how you shouldn't betray one for the other. I didn't know what that had to do with Bereishit, so it must have been something mentioned in her *haftarah*. Anyway, it started me thinking about Ben-o again, which I had managed not to do for a whole three and a half minutes. I wondered again if I'd made the right choice, being here.

Sheila and her mom wore matching lavender dresses. Who does that? Her dad even wore a purple tie. The reception was a festival of purpleness, too, just as I'd predicted. Purple tablecloths, purple balloons, purple everything. It made everyone look a little bruised, especially Sheila's relatives, who were all as pale as she was. In fact, they all looked exactly the same, like a clone colony. If you lined up her cousins from youngest to oldest, you would get a pretty good idea of what Sheila will look like in five, ten, and even twenty years. I, on the other hand, don't look like anyone in my family.

Seeing the lineup of Rosenberg-alikes made me think about the unit we'd done on genetics in science the previous week. Stuff like dominant and recessive traits that explain why someone like me could never inherit my dad's green eyes. Green eyes and attached earlobes and the ability to curl your tongue are recessive traits—meaning you have to inherit two copies of the gene, one from your father and one from your mother. Brown eyes and normal earlobes are dominant traits, meaning you only have to get them from one side or the other. The only thing I seemed to have inherited from both my parents was the ability to curl my tongue.

The thing about being mixed is that nobody ever says I look like this or that relative. And since I don't have any brothers or sisters, nobody looks like me either. I look at

Mum and Daddy and I try to see a resemblance, and it's as if I'm some kind of third species, not related to either of them. Rebecca and her mom have the exact same nose, and Ben-o's hair flops to the right (or at least it used to), same as his dad's. Sheila Rosenberg is a carbon copy of her mother. Me? I might as well be adopted, like Adam Greenspan.

I'm kind of like a vanilla milkshake with one pump of chocolate syrup—compared to white people I look brown, and to brown people I look white. Even my hair color is somewhere halfway between Daddy's sandy brown and Mum's chestnut. But it's neither one nor the other, just a nondescript shade in the middle. A color so boring, there's not even a crayon for it. Not even in the sixty-four pack.

I hung out with Missy Abrams while Rebecca was busy doing her best-friend-of-the-bat-mitzvah-girl stuff with Sheila. I also talked to Marina Cartwright, the eighth-grader from Robotics, for a while. I didn't even know she knew Sheila, but it turned out they're family friends, so her mom and three brothers were there, too.

Happily, the food wasn't purple, except for the little frosting flowers on the cake. Sheila called up Rebecca to light a candle, which is a big honor reserved for family and really close friends. I'm not gonna lie. I was jealous.

The truth is, I could learn to get along with Sheila Rosenberg, maybe even get on a first-name-only basis with her, if it meant saving my best-friendship with Rebecca. I could deal with anyone as long as I had my BFFs backing me up.

***

Sheila didn't show up for Hebrew school the next morning. It's kind of a tradition, not coming in the day after your own bar or bat mitzvah, but I was surprised anyway, because— she's Sheila Rosenberg. Rebecca said it was because she had a lot of out-of-town guests.

We were learning about the Holocaust, which is when the Nazis persecuted and killed twelve million people, including six million Jews. The subject is fascinating and awful at the same time. Some people did really amazingly heroic things, like the family that helped Anne Frank. It made me think, though: I mean, how could people let something like that happen in the first place? Rabbi said that was a good question.

He told us about some prisoners in a Nazi concentration camp who risked their lives to help a thirteen-year-old boy in their bunk have a secret bar mitzvah, and about another man who had a bar mitzvah when he was seventy, because he wasn't allowed to have one during the Holocaust. Rabbi says what makes the second story really special is that the man never lost faith.

It seemed incredible to me that someone could keep believing in God after living through something as terrible as that. And if he did, then why did I have any doubts whatsoever?

***

I finally worked up the nerve to approach the subject with Rabbi Aron on Monday. It was hard to know where to start.

"I don't know . . . how I feel about Judaism. The religious part," I confessed during my bat mitzvah lesson. For a moment I thought—wished, even—that he couldn't hear the question over the sound of my heart beating.

"Are you having a crisis of faith, Tara?" he asked kindly.

"I don't know," I said. In order to have a crisis of faith, I suspected you had to definitely have a faith first. I didn't even know if Mum and Daddy believed in God. Gran did. I mean, I assumed so, because all old people did. Rabbi said he wasn't sure about that.

"You do, right?" I asked him. "Believe in God?"

"Absolutely," he said.

"But how do you know?"

"Tara—I don't want to tell you what to think. You're far too smart to let me get away with that." Rabbi put his fingertips together. For a moment, I thought he was praying. "I ask only that you keep an open mind. And heart."

"How will *I* know?" I asked, my voice hardly a whisper.

"You'll know."

I bit my lip, almost afraid to ask. "Rabbi Aron . . ."

"Yes, Tara?"

"Do I have to believe in God to have my bat mitzvah?"

"It's not a requirement, no," Rabbi said gently. "Do you want to talk it out?"

That was a relief. Somehow not having to decide on the spot made me more willing to give it a chance. I had a thousand more questions, but I sat helpless, unable to put them into words. Rabbi seemed to sense my problem.

"Find comfort in your doubts, Tara," he said. "Only the weak are absolutely sure of everything."

"Really?"

"Really."

It was an interesting idea. But was it true? I mean, I was *absolutely sure* that two plus two made four. That wasn't weakness. And how was something as big and scary as not knowing if I believed in God supposed to be comforting?

"This is what you meant about dialectics, isn't it?" I said slowly. "That doubts are like questions."

"Precisely, my dear."

"Hmm," I said.

So it was okay to have questions, even about something so important. That was reassuring, I guess. It didn't make me any less good, or strong. It didn't make me any less Jewish. I didn't have to know everything. I just had to keep my heart and mind open. I could do that.

Maybe I did believe—or could. I wanted to. I could try. And maybe that was good enough. For a while.

Chapter 23

ara," Mum called. "Telephone, for you."

I'd heard it ring a moment earlier, but I figured it had to be for Mum or Daddy or, more likely, was a telemarketer.

Or, as it turned out—Sheila Rosenberg. Who, as Ben-o would say, kept turning up like a bad penny. I had no idea what to say to her.

"Hey, Sheila," I said, putting some fake enthusiasm into it, mostly because Mum thought Sheila was "lovely" and because I'd promised Rebecca I would continue to "try." It had been over two weeks since her bat mitzvah.

"What's new?" I asked, as if it were the most natural thing in the world for her to be calling me.

"I was wondering, would you and Rebecca like to come for a sleepover tomorrow?"

Me and Rebecca?

I was about to tell her she'd have to ask Rebecca herself, when she laughed and said, "Actually, Rebecca already said yes, this morning. But I wanted to ask you personally."

"Wh-why me?" I said, sounding rude to my own ears. "I mean, thanks and all, but—"

"I know you and I haven't always gotten along," Sheila said hurriedly, "but I like you, and I was happy you came to my bat mitzvah . . . and now that we share a best friend, I thought . . ."

I literally bit my tongue. *I know, I know,* I told myself. I had no right to be jealous. After all, I had two best friends, or at least I used to. Lately I felt like I was on the verge of losing them both.

But I *was* jealous. I still couldn't believe Rebecca had been besting it up with Sheila Rosenberg for so long, right under my nose. How had I not seen it? Now they were walking to school together, just the two of them, because Rebecca's block was "on Sheila's way." Whatever that meant. I was on the way, too, but I got the feeling Rebecca had been trying to keep us apart on purpose. Separate. Orderly. I should have been grateful to Sheila for reaching out, but I didn't trust her. Was she genuinely being nice to me or just doing this to get closer to Rebecca?

My two best friends, and their other best friends—it was starting to get crowded. I pondered which was worse— being the third wheel at a sleepover involving my own best friend or staying home imagining all the meaningful bonding they were doing without me. I knew I would be unhappy if I went and unhappy if I didn't.

In fact, I pondered it for so long, Sheila cleared her throat and asked if I was still there.

"Okay," I said.

"You'll come? Cool!" Sheila said. "We'll go to my house right after Hebrew school. My dad's making burgers out on the patio." She said this as if it was the height of sophistication, this rule-breaking barbecue in the winter.

"I'll be there," I said. "And, Sheila?"

"What?"

"Thanks."

"See you tomorrow," she said.

"On a school night?" Mum asked when I told her at dinner.

"No school Friday. Teacher workshops, remember?"

"Right," she said. "Well, I don't see why not! Sheila is a lovely girl."

"So you've mentioned."

$$* * *$$

At school the next day, Sheila was wearing a red-and-white-striped shirt and a cute new bracelet with tiny red and white crystals, like little diamonds.

"When'd you get that?" Rebecca asked at lunch, touching the crystal bracelet.

"Pretty, right?" said Sheila. "It's new."

"But it's not your birthday or anything."

"And it's not purple," I added.

Sheila shrugged.

Later, after Hebrew school, she ducked into the girls' bathroom with a small duffel bag. When she came out, she was wearing a different top, purple with small white flowers.

"Why'd you change?" I asked.

"No reason," she said, zipping up her coat. "Let's go. I'm starving."

Sheila lived in a brownstone, which was like a town house. It was only three blocks away from my building, but I hadn't been there since her birthday party sleepover in third grade, when Missy Abrams had an asthma attack and peed the bed all in the same night. A hundred years ago, the whole house belonged to one family, but now it was separated into small apartments. The Rosenbergs had the ground floor and the basement and the little garden out back, where Mrs. Rosenberg grew runty tomatoes and herbs like basil and parsley. Mum once gave her a cutting of cilantro from our kitchen window, so she used to grow that, too—except Sheila had that genetic thing where cilantro tastes like rusty soap to her, so Mrs. Rosenberg got rid of it. I kind of felt sorry for Sheila about that, because cilantro is delicious and nothing like rust or soap. She was also allergic to peanuts. Meena Auntie says only Americans can afford to have food allergies, and that's why no one in India is allergic to wheat or corn or peanuts or cilantro.

"We're home!" Sheila called, kicking the duffel bag into the back of the hall closet.

"Back here," her father called from the yard, where he was standing over the grill in a bulky sweater and wool cap, the kind Aravind Uncle would still be wearing in May.

"Is he *barbecuing*?" Rebecca asked, incredulous. "It's practically snowing."

"He always makes burgers on the grill. All year. It's kind of a family tradition."

"Where's your mom?" I asked.

"Away," Sheila said. "Visiting my aunt Julie for the week. It's her birthday. They're having a girls' weekend at the spa." The way she said it was more like "spaaahh," like she was making fun of them. Like she felt hurt being left out.

"How do you girls like your burgers?" Mr. Rosenberg called through the kitchen window.

With mango pickle on top, I thought, but I doubted he'd know what I was talking about.

"Medium," Rebecca called back.

"Medium rare for me, please, Mr. Rosenberg," I said.

"Medium rare is ready now, so just grab yourself a plate, Tara. You, too, Rebecca—yours'll be up in a minute." I noticed he didn't say, *Call me Avery*.

"Make mine well-done," Sheila reminded him.

"One burnt offering, coming up," Mr. Rosenberg joked. Sheila rolled her eyes.

The phone rang and Sheila ran to answer it. It was Mrs. Rosenberg. I saw Sheila slip off the red crystal bracelet and slide it into her pocket. "I have friends over for dinner," I heard her say. "The girls from Hebrew school—Rebecca and Tara."

"Feinstein," she said quietly, after a pause.

"You're up, Sheels," Mr. Rosenberg called. Sheila handed

him the phone through the window, and he handed her a plate. She sat down at the kitchen table with us and folded her hands to say a blessing. I was halfway through my burger already, but I put it down and stopped chewing while she said it. I swallowed and joined in on the "Amen." What's weird was that there were no adults at the table making her do it. It was like she *wanted* to. Her dad was still outside talking on the phone.

Sheila took the bracelet out of her pocket. "You wanna wear it?" she asked Rebecca.

"Okay," Rebecca said. She slipped it on her wrist to admire it, then slipped it off and handed it back to her. "It's pretty."

"You can have it."

"No, thanks," Rebecca said, seeming surprised by the offer.

Sheila shrugged and put it back in her pocket before her dad came back inside with the tray piled high with more burgers and veggie kabobs.

After dinner, Mr. Rosenberg excused Sheila from doing the dishes, but she did have to take out the garbage. Then we went downstairs to Sheila's room, which was—surprise—purple. Purple walls, purple carpet, purple overstuffed arm-chair, purple bedspread, purple lampshade. The only not-purple things in the whole room were six roller-ball pens, the nice kind, from Japan, laid out neatly on her desk.

"I *love* these pens!" said Rebecca. "My mom won't buy them for me, though, because I'd just lose them."

"Have one," said Sheila.

"Seriously?"

"Seriously."

"Won't your mom be upset?" I asked Sheila. "Those are expensive."

"Don't worry about it," Sheila said. "She'll never notice."

Rebecca suggested that we all get into our pj's and brush our teeth right away, so we could stay up as late as we wanted and fall asleep whenever. It would never occur to Rebecca to go to bed without brushing her teeth. We started to strip down right in the middle of the room. I stopped midsleeve when Rebecca nudged me, pointing with her chin at Sheila, who was pretending to be really interested in something on her desk. Keeping her back to us, she pulled on a flannel nightgown over her clothes and proceeded to undress backward, unhooking her bra—an honest-to-goodness bra—and pulling it out one sleeve, then wriggling out of her pants. It seemed like an awful lot of work. Why didn't she just take off her clothes first, like a normal person? I guessed she was self-conscious of her boobs, because she had them and Rebecca and I didn't. I did catch myself stealing looks in her direction and wondered what it was like to have them. Mainly they just looked uncomfortable. I finished putting on leggings and Daddy's old Tom Waits T-shirt that reached past my knees. Rebecca looked like she was getting ready to go out for a run instead of to bed, in an expensive-looking athletic jersey and matching track shorts.

"I'll be right back," Sheila said.

Rebecca brushed her hair and did ten sit-ups, but Sheila still didn't come back. We got our toothbrushes from our overnight bags and went to brush our teeth. The bathroom door was slightly open, so we pushed on it, not realizing Sheila was inside. We stood staring with our mouths open for what must have only been a second, but it seemed longer. Sheila had her hair up in a top ponytail and was using a hand mirror with a long plastic handle to see the back of her head reflected in the big mirror over the sink. And here's the thing—underneath all that black curly hair was a massive bald patch, red and angry, as if it had been scratched raw. Looking into the hand mirror, she reached up and found a few stray strands that she twirled twice around her finger and yanked out, hard, with a sick, ripping sound. There was hair all over the sink.

"What are you doing?" Rebecca shrieked.

Sheila jumped and dropped the hand mirror on the counter, where it clattered a few times but didn't break. She hastily took down the ponytail. Then she wiped up the hair around the sink with a tissue and buried it deep in the bathroom garbage. She walked out without saying anything, her face red. Rebecca and I brushed our teeth in absolute silence.

When we came back, Sheila was sitting on her bed with her head down and her eyes lowered.

I couldn't stop thinking about the hair-pulling fight we'd had in the beginning of the school year. I had a terrible thought. I sat down on the bed next to Sheila, trying to work up the nerve to ask.

"Did I do that?" I whispered, finally.

Sheila looked at me in surprise. "What, this? No." She bit her lip. "I do it to myself."

"But why?"

"I really don't know," she said.

After that, though, she smiled cheerfully and put on a stretchy headband, as if nothing had happened.

"Who wants to tell ghost stories before bedtime?" she said. She grabbed a flashlight and turned it on under her chin and then turned out the overhead lights. She really did look spooky for a second, with that pale skin and black hair and those eyes, but then she started to giggle, and that cracked up Rebecca, and then I started laughing, too, and pretty soon we forgot that we'd just learned that Sheila pulls her own hair out of her head when nobody's looking. I didn't know any ghost stories, though, so I listened to Sheila tell a lame one about a woman who always wore a wide velvet ribbon around her neck, which turned out to be because her head wasn't really attached to her body. On her wedding night, her new husband begged her to take off the ribbon, and when she finally did, her head rolled to the floor and she died for real. Then Rebecca told a camp story about a man named Cropsey, who got away with murdering his whole family and liked to reenact the event once a year by murdering campers and counselors who reminded him of his children and his wife. Rebecca swore it was true, but I pointed out that the camp would have been shut down ages ago, and besides, if everybody knew Cropsey's name, how come he wasn't in jail, and why was he allowed to run a camp? Rebecca said I spoiled the story.

"Whatever," I said.

After that, Sheila turned the lights back on and said, "Let's do manicures," and I knew it was because she'd gotten spooked by the Cropsey story and didn't want to be in the dark anymore. So she and Rebecca painted each other's toe-nails pink. I didn't feel like it, so I just picked up a book from Sheila's shelf and started to read, curled up in the purple armchair. Then I closed my eyes and pretended I was asleep. I felt like the intruder, even though Rebecca was *my* best friend.

Rebecca and Sheila stayed up a while longer, whispering and laughing, but not in a mean way, so I knew they weren't talking about me or excluding me on purpose, but I still felt lonely.

After they had been quiet for a while, I heard Rebecca whisper, "Why do you do that thing with your hair?"

"It's kind of hard to explain," Sheila said.

"Can I see?" Sheila lifted up her hair in back. Rebecca sucked in her breath. "You shouldn't do that," she said.

"I know," Sheila said quietly. "I can't help it."

"Do your parents know?"

"Kind of," she said. "Not really. Not exactly."

"Maybe if you put something on it . . ."

"Like what?"

"Like if you used Vaseline or something. Maybe you couldn't do it then—too slippery."

"Let's try that," Sheila said.

Opening one eye, I saw her pad to the bathroom and come back with a small jar.

"Yuck," I heard her say. "That feels gross. Forget it. It's not like I can go to school with Vaseline all over my head."

"I've never seen you do that in school," Rebecca said.

But then I remembered how she was always twirling her hair around her finger. Was that what she was really doing? I hoped nobody else noticed. That information could be really embarrassing in the wrong hands. Ryan Berger's, for example.

After that, it got quiet, because Rebecca fell asleep, so Sheila got up and took the book from my hand and pulled a blanket over me where I lay curled up, her purple teddy bear as my pillow. "Good night, Tara," she whispered, before she turned out the light and went to bed herself. When I woke up the next morning, I found the book tucked in my overnight bag with a note saying I could borrow it and give it back to her in school next week. There was even a bookmark holding my page.

Mr. Rosenberg made pancakes and let Sheila have a cup of real coffee, although it was more milk than coffee, judging by the color. I had a hot chocolate, only it was the instant kind with shriveled-up marshmallows that spring to life in hot water, not the real, shaved-chocolate kind that Daddy makes, which is the most delicious thing in the world, like drinking melted candy. Daddy sprinkles a little cinnamon on it, too, or sometimes a dash of chili pepper. We eat everything spicy at home. Nothing was spicy at Sheila's house, so by the time I got home, I was on a tear for some *masala* peanuts, devouring half a bag before Mum told me to stop or I was going to spoil my lunch.

Feeling lonely, I called Ben-o.

"How was Casa Rosenberg?" he asked. "Is everything purple inside?"

I laughed. "Yeah, mostly," I said. I decided not to tell him about Sheila's hair thing. It was a weird thing to know about somebody, and a weirder thing to gossip about. It would be like making fun of someone for something they can't help, like the shape of their ears, or a funny birthmark. I knew she wouldn't do it if she could help it, so I kept quiet, but keeping quiet about it also made me kind of not able to think of anything else to say. Ben-o finally said, "Are you still there?"

"Yeah, just thinking."

"About what?"

"Nothing. It was fun. Sheila's dad is really nice. Do you want to hang out at the park?" I said, all in one breath. "Shoot some hoops?"

"Can't," Ben-o said. "I'm meeting Jenna for chess practice."

"Oh," I said, closing my eyes. Then I had an idea. "Why don't you play chess in the park?"

"Too cold," Ben-o said.

He was right—it was way too cold for sitting in the park—but I was annoyed anyway.

"Whatever," I said. "Have fun."

"Tara—wait."

I listened without saying anything, but I didn't hang up. I could hear him scratching his crew-cut head.

"Do you want to come over later? Watch a movie?"

"Maybe," I said. Movie night was our *Saturday* thing.

"You can pick. You can bring over anything you want to watch."

"Okay," I said. "I guess."

"Cool. We'll call you when we're back—Jenna and me."

We again. Normally I'd be happy to hang out and watch a movie with him, even if it was only Friday. And Jenna's all right. But after the sleepover at Sheila's, I was feeling like a third wheel. Again.

"You know what?" I said. "Forget it. I'm too tired."

"Okay," Ben-o said, sounding doubtful. "Tomorrow, then—regular movie night. Me and you."

"Yeah," I said, and I hung up the phone.

Chapter 24

here's your binder?" I asked Ben-o as soon as I opened the door on Saturday.

"I didn't bring it." He shrugged. "It's your turn to pick."

"That's cool, but . . . maybe you should go get it," I said. "There's nothing here we'd both want to watch."

"Cool!" he said happily. "I'll be right back."

I went into the kitchen and made two bags of popcorn. When I came out, he was already there, squatting in front of the DVD player.

His hair was growing back a little. It looked slightly furry, like a teddy bear. I reached out to pet it and he jumped.

"What are you doing?" he said.

"I just wanted to touch it."

"Well, don't."

"Whatever," I said, feeling stung. "I get it. Your girl-friend won't like it."

"Who?"

"*Jenna,*" I said, exasperated.

"C'mon, Tara."

"You don't like Jenna?"

"Of course I like her. We're friends."

Friends.

"I mean—forget it."

Ben-o turned his back to me and rested his forehead on the wall.

"I like *you*," he mumbled, so quietly I was sure I wasn't meant to hear it. But I did. I pretended that I didn't, because—it terrified me. I mean, what if we tried being boyfriend and girlfriend and it didn't work out? Could we go back to being best friends again, like nothing had happened? I didn't think so. It was too much to risk. I couldn't afford to maybe lose another best friend.

"Do you want to watch the movie now?" I croaked.

"Okay," said Ben-o, moving away from the wall. His face had gone completely blank. Whatever he was feeling, he was keeping it to himself now.

He pressed the play button. I turned off the lights.

We sat next to each other on the couch, stiff as a couple of mannequins. I wondered if he was going to try to put his arm around me again, but he didn't. Which was weird. I mean, we both knew what was going on. Right? As soon as the movie was over, he got up to leave.

"Ben-o . . ." I faltered. I thought about what Rebecca had said, about me giving him mixed signals. I wasn't doing it on purpose. But I was confused, too. One minute he was my best friend; the next he wanted something else. And the minute after that, he was all about Jenna Alberts. I really didn't know what I was supposed to think. And now he was mad at me.

"Are you mad at me?" I asked.

Ben-o tilted his head to one side and thought about it. Longer than should have been necessary, I felt.

"I'm not mad at you," he said. "I'm a little mad at myself."

"Why?"

"Forget it," he said. "Really. Don't worry about it."

"Are you sure?"

"Yeah. I'm sure."

I didn't believe him.

Chapter 25

After my bat mitzvah lesson on Monday, I waited for Rebecca. It was too cold to wait outside, so I sat in the vestibule with my feet propped up on the radiator. I was doodling in my notebook when Sheila showed up.

"Hey," I said. "What are you doing here?" Obviously she no longer had lessons, since her bat mitzvah was long past.

"Waiting for Rivka," she said.

"Rivka?"

"Rebecca's Hebrew name." She giggled. "It's kind of a private joke between us."

First of all—of course I knew Rebecca's Hebrew name. And Sheila's, too, because of her bat mitzvah: Shoshana. But something about them having any sort of private joke bugged me, putting me in a dark mood. I tried to smile, but I'm sure it looked more like a sneer. Sheila remained oblivious.

"Want to join us?" she asked. "We're going shopping."

"Rebecca didn't mention it," I said.

"Well, come anyway. It'll be fun."

I doubted it, especially with those two—Preppy and Purply.

"Okay, but—can I drop off my stuff at home first?" I had checked out four books from the school library for my Robotics project and they were really heavy.

So we waited for Rebecca, and they both came home with me to drop off my books. Sheila had never been over before, so she kept touching everything in my room and asking, "What's this?" and "What's that?"

Rebecca rubbed Ganesha's belly. Sheila stopped short. "What's *that*?" she asked.

"That's Ganesha," Rebecca informed her. "He's a Hindu god. It's good luck to rub his belly. Try it."

"Why do you have it?" Sheila asked, turning to me.

"My grandfather gave it to me."

"But I thought you said your mom is Jewish."

"She is," I said, starting to get mad. "How many times—"

"I know, I know," Sheila said quickly. "But . . . why does she let you have idols?"

"*Idols?*"

"False gods," Sheila said.

"I know what it means," I snapped. After all, it's right there in the Ten Commandments: *You shall have no other God except me.* But something in the way she said "false gods" really got under my skin.

"I never thought of it like that," Rebecca said, drawing her hand away.

Neither had I, really. If I'd thought about it at all, it was like kissing a *mezuzah*, or pouring an extra glass of wine for the prophet Elijah to drink on Passover. A ritual. My Nanaji thing. Not idolatry.

Not too long ago, I'd vowed not to let being Jewish and having a bat mitzvah in any way diminish Nanaji's memory. I hadn't expected it to get complicated.

"I don't want to talk about this," I said. "Let's go." I grabbed my coat and stomped out, Rebecca and Sheila trailing behind.

✳ ✳ ✳

I was still brooding while Rebecca and Sheila window-shopped on Broadway. I was grumpy and hungry and my feet hurt from walking around in the cold. We passed the store where Sheila had gotten her crystal bracelet, so of course Rebecca wanted to go in and have a look.

"If I were going to buy one, I'd get this one," Rebecca said, holding up one with little blue and pink crystals. "It's a lot like yours, but different. Then we wouldn't have the exact same one."

"We could swap sometimes," Sheila said.

"Cool," said Rebecca.

"How about this one for you, Tara?" Sheila said, holding up a pretty turquoise one.

"Not my style," I said. "Even if I had the money, I'd rather buy a game."

"Like Monopoly?"

"Like Killer Zombie Princess Three." Actually, I'd buy

Res-Q Robots. I said Killer Zombie Princess just to shock Sheila, and it worked, judging from her expression.

"You're both idiots," said Rebecca mildly. She sounded so much like the old Rebecca that I smiled, but Sheila actually looked hurt. Like no one had ever called her an idiot in a friendly way. Which was kind of sad.

"Anyway," Rebecca said with a sigh, "I don't have the money either."

"Let me get it for you," said Sheila.

"Nah," said Rebecca. "Maybe for my birthday, which isn't until forever."

A block away from the store, Sheila stopped Rebecca and said, "I have a surprise for you."

"What?" Rebecca asked.

"Shut your eyes and hold out your hand."

Rebecca did, and Sheila placed the blue and pink crystal bracelet in her palm. Rebecca's eyes flew open. She looked like she might be sick.

"Sheila! What did you do?"

"Consider it an early birthday present."

"But you didn't pay for this. You have to take it back."

"Too late," Sheila said. "If we go back now, we risk getting caught."

We?

"I'm taking it back," Rebecca said, her voice shaking.

"Rebecca, don't—"

"I'll take it back," I said, snatching the bracelet from Rebecca.

"Hold up. We're coming with you," Rebecca said, dragging Sheila by the arm.

I walked ahead of both of them, but when I reached the revolving door, I felt a flicker of panic. I hesitated for just a second before I pushed my way into the store. I was just reaching to put the bracelet back on the jewelry counter when I felt a large hand on my shoulder. The security guard already had Rebecca and Sheila in tow.

* * *

The back office was depressing, with harsh, buzzing fluorescent lights and no windows. The heat was up so high, it felt like there was no air in the room. The security guard— Mr. R. Gregory, according to his badge—reached into a drawer and pulled out a stack of forms. He didn't look at us even once as he began to fill them out.

"You first, curly," he said. He took down Sheila's name, her parents' names, and her home phone number. He picked up the phone and called.

You can tell a lot about a person by the way their parents react to a crisis. Mrs. Rosenberg was shouting so loudly that Mr. R. Gregory had to hold the phone away from his ear. He rubbed his eyes as if he had a terrible headache.

When he called Rebecca's house next, her dad answered. We couldn't hear him at all, but that's because Mr. Goldstein never raised his voice, ever. That can sometimes be scarier. Then it was my turn.

"Name?"

"Tara Feinstein."

Mr. R. Gregory finally looked up, a skeptical look on his face. "No, really," he said.

"Yes, really," I said.

He shook his head, but he wrote it down. After I recited my phone number, I clammed up. If there's one thing I learned from Meena Auntie, it's keep your trap shut until your lawyer arrives. Or whoever. As he punched in the number, I silently willed Daddy to pick up the phone. *Not Mum, not Mum*, I prayed. I must be the luckiest person in the world, because miraculously, it wasn't Mum or Daddy who answered. It was Gran. I almost smiled with relief.

"Don't you lay a finger on those children," I heard her squawk, as loudly as if she were there in the room. "Are you listening to me? I'll be there just as soon as I can be."

It seemed to take forever for the grown-ups to arrive. Sheila stared at the floor, twisting a strand of hair around her finger, looking paler than her usual skim milk. Only Rebecca couldn't stop talking, from nerves.

"I'm never getting into law school with a criminal record," she moaned.

"You're a juvenile," Sheila said. "It doesn't count."

"Hey, Sheila?" I said, breaking my vow of silence. "Shut up."

"I'm just pointing out the facts. It's not like she's gonna get the electric chair."

"She didn't *do* anything."

"I know," said Sheila.

"This is all your fault," I hissed.

"I know."

"Then shut up."

Mrs. Rosenberg was the first to arrive, then Rebecca's dad, then Gran—along with Vijay, who could hardly contain his joy at my predicament.

"What are you doing here?" I whispered.

"Yo, I'm your ride, homie," he said, dangling the car keys.

Gran smacked his behind. "I told you not to talk." At least she didn't hit him in the head. But then again, he's not actually her grandson.

"Mr. Feinstein, I suppose?" Mr. R. Gregory said to Vijay sarcastically.

"Nah, man, the name's Mehta," said Vijay. "Bro—didn't you used to be at Modell's?"

"Didn't I once arrest you for stealing a soccer ball?"

"That was me!" Vijay said, excited, as if this were a reunion instead of the worst day of my life. He smiled and extended his hand enthusiastically, but Mr. R. Gregory refused to shake it.

"Vijay, go wait in the car," Gran said.

I'll say this for Sheila: she copped to it right away. As soon as Vijay left and the rest of the adults settled down, she admitted everything, including how I had been trying to return what she had taken. Sheila may have been a thief, but she wasn't a liar. And she wasn't taking the rest of us down with her.

Mrs. Rosenberg was awful.

"Stop DOING that!" she snapped, seeing Sheila twisting a strand of hair. Sheila put her hands in her lap and looked down. "What has gotten into you?"

Sheila shrugged.

"Are you on drugs, Sheila?" Mrs. Rosenberg asked.

"No!" Sheila wailed. "God."

"We've given you everything . . ."

"As long as it's *purple*," Sheila whispered, too quietly for her mother to hear.

"You had only to ask."

"That's the POINT!" Sheila shrieked hysterically. "I don't want to ASK. And I HATE PURPLE!"

Mrs. Rosenberg looked stunned. "Sheila—"

"Take it easy, Phyllis," Rebecca's dad said.

Mr. R. Gregory cleared his throat. "Can we get back on track here?"

"Yes, please," said Rebecca's dad.

We signed papers saying we'd never enter the store again, at least until we turned eighteen. Like I'd ever go in there again. Ever. We each had to write an apology letter to the store manager. I didn't know what to write—*I'm sorry my best friend's new best friend stole a dumb bracelet and I tried to return it but I got caught?* Then Mr. R. Gregory handed Mrs. Rosenberg a copy of the "incident report" and told her to do a better job keeping an eye on Sheila. Mrs. Rosenberg looked ready to kill him. We were all free to go.

✳ ✳ ✳

"What I fail to comprehend," Mum kept saying, "is why you called your grandmother instead of *me*."

"I didn't," I said. "I gave the guard our number. Gran just happened to answer the phone."

"You should have called my mobile, Tara, as you know very well. And you—" she said, turning a terrible eye on Gran. "You should know better."

Gran actually looked sheepish. "You're right, Rita. I shouldn't have stuck my nose in." Mum raised an eyebrow. "But the child was terrified, and I just—instinct took over. I'm sorry."

"I was a little terrified," I admitted this time.

"Of course you were!" Gran cried. "They had no right to detain you, do you know that? A twelve-year-old without her parents?"

"Almost thirteen," I pointed out.

"I'm not sure that's true, Ma," Daddy said.

"Ask Meena!" Gran snapped. "See what an attorney has to say about it. You ought to sue them for all they're worth. It's that Sheila Whatzername. There's something wrong with that one. All you have to do is look at her."

"Gran!"

"What?"

"If someone said that about me, it would be racist."

"Who's a racist? I'm a Jew, she's a Jew. I'm telling you that girl has a screw loose."

"Mr. R. Gregory didn't believe my name was Tara Feinstein," I told her. "Because I'm brown."

"Tara . . ." Mum said.

"Brown?" Gran yelled. "Who's brown? My father was as brown as you."

"Really?"

"A Sephardic!" she said. "Real classy. My mother was the Ashkenaz."

"Ma—" Daddy said, rubbing the bridge of his nose. He sounded exhausted. Gran is always saying nonsensical things like that, as if you're supposed to know that Sephardim are a classy brown people.

"And involving Vijay? I will never hear the end of it from Meena," Mum added.

"He was certainly in his element," Gran muttered.

"I was so worried, Tara," Mum said, ignoring Gran. "To think that you might have stolen something . . ."

"Mum," I said, "you raised me better than that."

"All I'm saying is, you need to think about the company you keep."

"No fair!" I said. "You're the one who's always telling me what a *lovely* girl Sheila is, and why can't I be nicer to her, blah blah blah blah blah."

"Perhaps you are a better judge of character than I am after all," Mum said. I was disconcerted by the compliment, because—really? Sheila did this one dumb-headed thing and I wasn't supposed to be her friend anymore? That was harsh. Didn't everyone deserve a second chance?

* * *

Sheila's parents made her come over and apologize in person. They came to us first. Probably as a practice run for Rebecca's, I thought.

"What do you say, Tara?" Daddy said, nudging me.

"I accept your apology," I recited, just as I'd promised Daddy I would.

"Thanks," Sheila said, looking truly relieved.

"Well," Mrs. Rosenberg said, folding her hands primly in her lap. "Now that's cleared up. Tara, is there something you'd like to say to Sheila in return?"

"Not really," I said. I had no idea what she was getting at. Sheila looked like she might die of embarrassment. She shook her head at me furiously, as if to tell me this wasn't her idea, or her fault.

"Wouldn't you like to apologize to Sheila for hitting her?" Mrs. Rosenberg prompted me.

"*Hitting* her?" Mum cried. "Tara? What is she talking about?"

Why was she bringing this up now? That fight was ancient history. Mum didn't know about it, and I'd been trying to keep it that way. I said the only thing I could think of:

"She started it."

"Mom," Sheila whined. "You promised . . ."

"Did you or did you not hit her?" Mum persisted.

"She *bit* me."

"After you pushed me," Sheila said.

"After you trash-talked my mother!"

"Girls!"

Mrs. Rosenberg looked dismayed. "Sheila didn't tell me that part," she admitted.

"Mom, you weren't supposed to say anything," Sheila said. "You promised me."

"Perhaps we should leave it to the girls to work it out," Daddy said.

"We already did," Sheila and I said at the same time.

"Nevertheless," said Mum, "Tara will apologize to Sheila."

"I will?"

"You will," Mum said. Unlike Sheila's parents, though, mine weren't going to make me do it in front of them. Mrs. Rosenberg waited expectantly, but Mum intervened. "Let's give the girls their privacy, shall we? Coffee's ready." She herded the adults into the kitchen.

I waited for them to leave before I exploded.

"If you even THINK I'm going to apologize again—"

"No, I'm sorry," Sheila said. "For telling my mom all that. I should have known she wouldn't keep quiet. I told her that a long time ago, before we were friends. I begged her not to call your mom."

Friends. I couldn't help smiling. Sheila was all right. Messed up, but all right.

"She just saved it up for a rainy day." Sheila snorted. "Are you going to be in trouble?"

"I don't know," I said. "Probably. But it's not your problem. Just tell your mom I apologized, okay?"

"Okay." She sighed. "We're going to Rebecca's next. Wish me luck."

"Good luck," I said. "You'll need it."

"Do you think she'll forgive me?"

I hesitated. Knowing Rebecca, it would take her a long time to get over this. If she ever did.

"Eventually," I said. I didn't have the heart to tell her otherwise.

"Sheila," her dad called. "Ready?"

"Coming!" she called back.

Chapter 26

ebecca called early the next morning to say she wanted to walk to school with Ben-o and me. I filled Ben-o in quickly before we got to her block.

Ben-o didn't believe me. "Sheila *Rosenberg*?"

"You know another Sheila?" I sighed wearily. It really was hard to believe. Sheila Rosenberg, the self-appointed moral compass of the seventh grade, a petty thief. She'd redeemed herself by confessing so Rebecca and I wouldn't get in trouble. Still—

"She's clearly working out some unresolved issues," I said, quoting Mum.

"Like what?"

I flashed to her hair pulling, but I didn't say it out loud.

"Just stuff," I said.

Rebecca was already waiting on her corner when we got there, and immediately she started bad-mouthing Sheila. I mean, I got why she was still mad, but just the previous night, she had accepted Sheila's apology, before God and her parents and everyone. A deal was a deal.

"All her talk about idolatry and whatnot, and the whole time she's been breaking an even bigger commandment." She paused for effect, but when neither Ben-o nor I said anything, she went on. "Um, *hello*? You shall not *steal*?" Rebecca blew hair out of her eyes viciously.

"I get it, it stinks," I said. "Anyway, she's not going to shoplift anymore. I heard Mum telling Gran that Sheila's going to get therapy."

"Retail therapy?" Ben-o snickered.

"That's not nice," I said, laughing anyway. "But seriously, that's good, right?"

"Yeah," said Rebecca. "Maybe she'll stop pulling her hair out, too."

"Stop it, Rebecca!" I said, tilting my head toward Ben-o. It was mean of her to bring it up in front of him, and of course he got curious. I mean, who wouldn't be?

"What are you talking about?" he asked.

"Nothing," I said, glaring at both of them. But Rebecca told him the whole story in one breath, about the sleepover and how we found out that Sheila is a hair puller.

"That's gross," Ben-o said mildly. "Tara never told me that part." I knew he wouldn't start spreading rumors all over school, but it was still mean of Rebecca. Just then, I caught sight of Sheila up ahead, walking by herself. I knew she must have seen me and Rebecca together, and maybe even heard us laughing, because she was walking rigidly with her head down, refusing to look in our direction. Suddenly I felt sorry for her, and angry at Rebecca for putting me in this spot. It hadn't been my idea to be friends with Sheila Rosenberg in the first place, and now it wasn't my idea to stay mad at her. Right then, I didn't want to deal with either of them, or Ben-o. I just wanted to be alone for once. At the corner, I pretended to wave to a largish group of kids from our school on the other side of the street. I told Rebecca and Ben-o that I had to exchange math notes with "someone." Then I crossed the street and walked the rest of the way to school by myself.

Chapter 27

Almost before I knew it, it was November, and Diwali was here. Meena Auntie's annual Diwali potluck would be on Saturday, so on Friday Daddy did a trial run of his contribution—potato *latkes* with tamarind chutney and yogurt sauce. Mum and I pronounced it a huge success, much better than the *chana-jor-garam*-crusted chicken wings he attempted last Diwali, which in theory should have been delicious but actually were just soggy and awkward to eat.

Diwali got me thinking about Nanaji, and missing him terribly. It was his favorite holiday, probably because of all the sweets and the *patakas*—fireworks. Diwali is like Hanukkah, Christmas, and the Fourth of July all rolled into one. And when Diwali and Hanukkah happen only a couple of weeks apart, like this year—Diwalikkah jackpot! Bonus gifts. Which was all great except for the fact that my bat mitzvah was coming up fast, a couple of days before Hanukkah, so I was too nervous to completely enjoy myself.

It was not that I wasn't ready—I had my Torah and *haftarah* readings down and my speech pretty much memorized. I said it once a day in front of the bathroom mirror just to make sure I hadn't forgotten any of it.

Diwali and Hanukkah are both called the Festival of Lights, which I always thought was a very interesting coincidence. Hanukkah is called the Festival of Lights because when the Jews reclaimed the Holy Temple in Jerusalem—after the Maccabees drove out the Greeks—they thought they only had enough oil to light the menorah for one day, but the oil miraculously lasted eight days—enough time to make more. Which was a pretty cool miracle, I guess. I learned that in Hebrew school.

I didn't exactly know why Diwali was the Festival of Lights, so I looked it up on the Internet, and it turned out there were at least two different explanations. I laughed— Jews weren't the only people who liked to leave things open to interpretation. In one explanation, the lights were to welcome Lakshmi, the goddess of wealth, into your home. Kind of like opening the door for Elijah on Passover, I guess, but with a cash incentive. Actually, you were supposed to pray to Ganesha, the remover of obstacles, first, to make sure your path to prosperity and well-being was clear. Which was pretty smart. In the second version, the lamps and firecrackers were to celebrate the return of Rama after he defeated the demon king Ravana.

When I had mentioned the Festival of Lights thing to Rabbi Aron on Monday, it turned out he already knew that. Which was cool. I didn't know they taught Hinduism and stuff in rabbi school. I would have thought they'd be too busy reading the Torah and Talmud, but Rabbi said everyone in the seminary is required to study comparative religions.

As far as I knew, Hinduism didn't have anything equivalent to a bat mitzvah, so I wondered what Nanaji would have thought about me having one. He had a pretty open mind about stuff, kind of like Rabbi Aron. I bet he would have loved it, actually. Especially the candy table.

After dinner, I tapped on Mum's office door.

"It's open," she called.

"Mum, I just wanted to know . . . Were Nani and Nanaji . . . Were they—religious?"

Mum studied my face for a long moment before she answered me.

"Yes, but maybe not in the way you think," she said finally. "I would say Papa was a very spiritual person—he thought . . . that everyday things were holy. You remember how he loved birds, for example?"

I did remember, actually. He used to take me around his garden in India, pointing out all the creatures hiding in the trees and shrubbery.

"Show yourself!" he once shouted at a flowering tree, and a small green bird poked its head out of the thick leaves. *"Ach-cha!"* Nanaji had said with some satisfaction. "You have come back."

"Who are you talking to, Papa?" Meena Auntie had asked.

"It is my friend *chhota basant*—this little green bird has kept away all the winter."

"Oh-ho, scolding the small birds," Auntie said with amusement.

"Why not?" said Nanaji. "They only will listen to an old man such as me."

"You're not so old, Nanaji," I said, tugging on his leg.

"Not so old? How does one only this high judge the age of a man?"

I buried my face against his leg, and he reached down to swing me to his shoulders.

Nanaji was a big man, which was kind of funny, because Nani was tiny—shorter than Gran, even. And equally feisty.

"Only thing I am missing nowadays is the poor sparrow," he said once I was securely seated on his shoulders. "They are no more in India."

"This is not true," Meena Auntie said, sucking her teeth.

"It is true, all right," Nanaji rejoined. "The skies used to be filled with sparrows, but they have all disappeared."

"All of them?" I asked, skeptical, tracing a pattern on the top of his head with my index finger.

"*Arrey, beta,*" he said patiently. "Not like 'poof.' Over time, with the pollution, they have all gone. Here as well as all the cities in Europe."

Meena Auntie sucked her teeth again.

"Where are they?" Nanaji insisted. "Listen. What *cheep-chip* is there? Once, you couldn't sleep for all the sparrows in the guava tree."

"Such noise," Meena Auntie agreed.

"Now I can sleep away the whole morning until the *dud-hwallah* comes shouting."

It was true. The garden was strangely quiet. You don't realize how loud silence can be until the birds have gone away.

Later, though, Mum and Auntie and I went to the big American-style mall on the outskirts of the city, and as we walked past the parking garage, we saw hundreds of small birds swooping toward one enormous tree. They were moving so fast, it was impossible to see them clearly. More and more went in among the leaves, and none came out. The noise coming from the tree was unbelievably loud, as if every small bird in the world had decided to inhabit that one tree. I peered into the branches. "Sparrows! Mummy, look. Sparrows!"

Mum was distracted. I tugged the loose end of her *dupatta*. "Sparrows."

"Yes, Tara, I hear them."

"Oh-ho," Meena Auntie said, holding her head. "Such noise."

"But remember Nanaji said—"

No one was listening.

When we got home, I ran straight to Nanaji to tell him what I had seen. I was speaking very fast and he couldn't make out half of what I was saying. "Sparrows!" I repeated.

"No sparrows in India," Nanaji mused, catching only the word.

"But, Nana! I saw them."

"In a book?"

"In a tree! A great big tree. There were hundreds of them in this one tree, maybe thousands. A tree. At the mall."

"They were shopping?" he teased.

"Nana-*jiiiiii!*" I stamped my foot.

"Okay, *beta*, okay," Nanaji said, swinging me high. "It seems all the sparrows of India are living in this tree of yours. This must have made quite some racket, your sparrow tree."

"Such noise!" Meena Auntie said again.

Vijay, standing behind her, held his ears and rolled his eyes in imitation. I didn't care, though, because I knew Nanaji believed me.

"God's self must be watching over this tree," he said.

Spiritual. Was that what Mum meant? It was a comforting thought, and I kind of liked the sound of it. If spiritual meant being kind to animals, and being adventurous, and loving flowers and trees and every kind of food, and having an open heart and mind—then maybe I was spiritual, too.

* * *

On Saturday, Daddy rented a car so we could transport Gran and her big soup pot to Meena Auntie's—the only place in the world where Diwali is celebrated with a vat of matzoh ball soup. It's really supposed to be for Passover, but Gran makes it for all special occasions. She has to make it twice in November—once for Thanksgiving ("just like the Pilgrims ate," Daddy always jokes) and once for Diwali, because Meena Auntie loves it so.

Every year, besides family, Meena Auntie invites every single Indian she knows, whether they are Hindu or not, and they all come. Like Aisha Khan and her family—they're Bengali, and Muslim. Meena Auntie says even though they might not have had much in common in India, it's different here, because "in *Amreeka*, we are all brown." That always makes Daddy cringe, even though everyone else laughs.

Anyway, Meena Auntie and Mrs. Khan being friends was awesome, because everyone knows Bengalis make the best milk sweets in the world, and Mrs. Khan made the best Bengali sweets in all of New York: light, sweet *rasgullas* and creamy *rasmalai* (which she pronounced in the Bengali way—"*rosha*gullas" and "*rosh*malai") and her best thing—*mishti doi*—a sweet, custardy yogurt pudding. And Aisha's cool. It was nice to have someone my age to hang with instead of Vijay and his pothead friend Biff. I usually brought Rebecca, but this time she had to go to yet another family bar mitzvah. Which was just as well, because if I had to spend the whole day listening to her complain about Sheila, I would surely go mad.

Meena Auntie brought out two trays of her famous potato-pea samosas, which she only makes once or twice a year, since they are such a pain in the *tuchis* (a word she learned from Gran).

"Joshua, see here, I have made this second batch extra bland for your sensitive American stomach," Meena Auntie said, patting his shoulder. "The chilies and onions on the side." I saw Daddy grit his teeth. He loves spicy food, but

Auntie can never get used to that idea, all because of that time we all went to India together and Daddy got food poisoning. Twice. It had nothing to do with the food being spicy, but once Auntie gets an idea in her head, she can't let it go. Like a dog with a bone. Gran doesn't eat Indian food anymore, spicy or not, ever since her gallbladder surgery. She says even the clarified butter gives her heartburn.

It was a truly awesome feast. It would have been even more awesome if mangoes were in season, but Mum had solved that problem by bringing five pints of Häagen-Dazs mango sorbet, which is the next best thing. Besides, if there had been fresh mangoes, both Meena and Mum would spend the whole day complaining about how they weren't as good as Indian ones. And so expensive, too.

"Imagine," Meena Auntie said to Mum. "One hundred fifty rupees for an unripe Mexican mango? What would Papa say?"

Mum just laughed, but I knew exactly what Nanaji would say, from all those times we bought peeled mangoes on the way to Central Park. First of all, he would try to haggle, the way he was used to doing at home. He could never understand why the New York City street vendors were unwilling to bargain with him.

"That price?" he would say. "For one only?"

"*Sí*, for one," the lady would say. Of course Nanaji would buy it anyway—two, in fact. One for each of us.

All the way to the park he would mutter complaints.

Nevertheless, he would devour the whole thing down to the stringy pit, and then he would finish mine, too.

"Calling this a mango? In India, from your grandmother, this lady would be running for her life." Which was so true. The *fruitwallah* had been terrified of Nani, all four-feet-two of her.

"Hey," said Aisha, nudging me now.

"Hey," I said.

"Are you going to Ryan Berger's bar mitzvah?"

"Are you?" I asked, surprised. "So he really did apologize to you, then?"

"Yeah." She laughed. "It was awkward. But he meant it, so yeah. I forgave him."

"*That's* cool of you."

"So you don't have to beat him up again."

Meena Auntie was coming out of the kitchen then with another tray of samosas. "Who is beating up people?" she asked.

"Nobody," Aisha and I both answered. Auntie paused to give us a stern look, setting the tray on the buffet table.

Aisha pointed to the big pot of soup steaming in the middle of the table. "Is that the weird soup your grand-mother makes?"

Meena Auntie and I both laughed.

"Try some," Meena Auntie coaxed, ladling some into a bowl. "You've never had anything like it."

Aisha sampled it. "It's good," she said.

"So light and fluffy, *nahi*?" said Meena Auntie.

"A little bland, though," Aisha said.

"It's supposed to be, actually," I told her.

Auntie shot a furtive glance toward Gran, who was busy showing Mrs. Khan a new knitting trick. She reached into the pocket of her *salwar* and brought out a little jar of cayenne pepper. When she was sure Gran wasn't looking, she sprinkled some into Aisha's bowl and dumped the rest into the soup pot, along with a small handful of chopped onions and green chilies from the bowl next to the samosas.

Aisha sampled the soup again and nodded. "That works."

"Our little secret," Auntie said, winking.

Soon, Mr. Khan helped himself to a warm samosa.

"Aisha is looking very grown-up," Meena Auntie observed.

"Yes," he agreed, placing a hand on Aisha's shoulder. "Soon it will be time to find her a husband."

"Seriously?" I whispered to Aisha.

"Sheesh, Dad, I'm twelve," she complained, turning red.

Mrs. Khan looked up and smiled. "*Arrey, beta*, not today," she said soothingly. "You should have your education at least."

Aisha threw her hands up in exasperation. It was a good thing she had finished her soup.

"Yo, girl, I'll marry you," Vijay offered.

"No, thanks," she said.

"I thought you was already married, Vee—to Tara," Aisha's older brother, Salman, said, cracking himself up.

"Homes, that's disgusting," Vijay cried, shoving him.

"T's my little sis." He touched the *rakhi* on his wrist as evidence.

"You *must* love her, dude, to wear that mangy thing," Salman commented.

"You wish you had this."

"Vijay's your *brother*?" Aisha asked, with a mix of revulsion and admiration.

"Cousin," I said. "It's a Punjabi thing."

Gran served herself a bowl of soup.

"Joshua," I heard her say, "there's something wrong with the soup."

"Ma—there's nothing wrong with your matzoh ball soup."

"Taste this," she said, putting a spoonful into his mouth.

"Ma—"

"Don't talk with your mouth full."

"—there's never anything wrong—" Just then, Daddy started to cough, and he couldn't stop.

"What is it, son? Speak to me. Are you choking?"

Daddy held up one finger while he tried to catch his breath.

"Green chilies," he said, wheezing. "I swallowed one."

"Chilies? What are you, *meshugge*?" Gran yelled, but then she turned to Meena Auntie sharply. Auntie looked around desperately, but no one was going to save her. Aisha hid behind her mother.

"I didn't do anything, Ruthie-jee," Meena Auntie lied.

"Yes, she did," Vijay said. "I saw her."

"Meena!" said Mum. "How could you?"

Aravind Uncle ladled some soup into a bowl, tasted it, and delivered his ruling: "This soup has been souped up," he said.

There was a moment of stunned silence, and then an explosion of laughter—no one remembered hearing Uncle's voice before, and here he was cracking a joke. He lapsed back into silence, smiling serenely, while we all laughed.

Only Gran was not amused.

"Meshuggeners," she muttered.

"Poor Joshua," Meena Auntie whispered to Mrs. Khan. "He can't take the strong spices. Very delicate stomach he has."

Daddy left the room in a huff. I caught Mum's eye and we both giggled.

I wandered over to the fireplace and stood watching this strange *masala* that was my life. I couldn't help smiling. My *desi mishpacha*, I thought—my crazy Indian Jewish family— was a lot like Gran's souped-up matzoh ball soup. Traditional and spicy at the same time. Who else could say that?

I thought again of Nanaji, how much he would have approved of Auntie's mixed-up little Punjabi-Bengali-American-Hindu-Muslim-Jewish Diwali potluck. And then I knew—it was going to be okay. More than okay. I could be Indian American and Jewish American all at the same time. I could have my bat mitzvah and still honor Nani and Nanaji. I was a spiritual person, like Nanaji. I was just me, and there was nothing weird about that. Nothing at all.

Chapter 28

After Ryan Berger's bar mitzvah ceremony, Mr. Khan drove Aisha, Rebecca, Ben-o, and me to the reception, which was at a fancy catering hall on the far Upper West Side.

Ryan had changed out of his suit but was still wearing the fancy French-cuffed shirt and dorky red-and-white polka-dot bow tie from the morning—the ones he'd gotten at Macy's that time we ran into each other. His thick mat of brown hair was plastered down with something hard like varnish.

"You look fancy," Aisha said to him on the receiving line.

"Thanks," said Ryan, tugging at his collar. "The tie's a little tight. I tied it myself."

I have to admit, I was actually a little impressed by that.

There were *tons* of people there, because Ryan had invited everyone from both Hebrew school classes, plus our homeroom and the entire Robotics Club. Surprisingly, after that thing in the park, he'd even invited Ben-o, who I think showed up just for me. Or maybe Jenna Alberts.

Sheila was there, too, even though she hadn't invited Ryan to hers. Rebecca still wasn't talking to her, which was awkward. I was seated next to Missy Abrams, but Rebecca made her switch seats so we could sit together and to put some space between herself and Sheila. Ben-o sat across the table from me, with Adam.

I was happy Ben-o was there. I'd been invited to so many bar mitzvahs that most of my Saturdays were booked. A couple of times recently, I'd fallen asleep afterward and missed movie night. And I'd never made it up to him for missing his chess thing. Although he had taken Jenna, so— *You're welcome.*

"You were right about Ryan's tie," I told Adam.

"Dorky, right?"

"Very. But cool, too."

Ben-o was listening. "What are you guys talking about?" he asked.

"Ryan's tie. I ran into him at Macy's the day he got it."

"You were at Macy's?"

"With Mum. Shopping for dumb dresses." I crossed my eyes.

"You never mentioned you ran into Berger."

"I was there, too," Adam chimed in.

"So . . . what? Did you help him pick out his Pee-wee Herman tie?"

"Don't be stupid," I said. "We just had ice cream."

Ben-o stared at me silently.

We all danced while the main-course dishes were being

cleared away. After a couple of fast songs, the deejay switched to a slow one so the old people could dance. Some kids left the floor, but Ben-o put out his hand.

"May I have this dance?"

I smiled. Friends again. Ben-o put his hands on my back, and I put mine on his shoulders, and we started swaying awkwardly.

After only a minute, Ryan tapped Ben-o on the shoulder.

"Can I cut in?" he asked. For a second, I thought he meant like cutting in line, and I was confused. Then I realized he wanted to dance with me, too.

"No way," Ben-o said.

"Come on," he insisted. "It's my bar mitzvah."

Ben-o couldn't say no to that. Not that anyone had asked *me*.

Ryan was a way better dancer than Ben-o. We kept colliding, but truthfully it was mostly my fault, because I kept forgetting I had to step back when he stepped forward and vice versa.

"You're supposed to let me lead," he said, stepping on my feet.

"Ow," I said.

I stared over his shoulder at Ben-o, who was looking down at the floor and scuffing his foot like a bull about to charge. I kept hoping he would look up and see that this wasn't my idea. But then I saw Jenna Alberts tap him on the shoulder and whisper something in his ear. *His backup*, I thought bitterly. Maybe he really did like her better and had just been using me for target practice.

But then Jenna gave him a little shove back onto the dance floor.

Without warning, Ryan tried to twirl me, and I got tangled up in my own feet.

"You could have given me a heads-up," I complained.

Ben-o walked up to us slowly, turning around once or twice to look at Jenna, who waved him forward. He tapped Ryan's shoulder.

"I'm cutting back in," he said.

"Why don't we ask Tara who she wants to dance with?" Ryan said, gripping my arm.

Well, it's about time someone asked me, I thought.

I bit my lip. "I want to dance with Ben-o."

Ryan looked surprised, but he let go of my arm and stepped away. Ben-o slid in to take his place. Before things could get any more awkward, Jenna saved the day by running up and asking Ryan to dance.

"Careful, Benny," he said in a loud whisper. "She's a toe breaker."

Jenna did an expert dance move that landed them about ten feet away. Ben-o and I were alone.

So I had been wrong about them—Jenna and Ben-o. That should have been a relief. But instead I felt another stab of envy at the way she had taken charge, known exactly what to do. Like a best friend should.

Also, I felt a little bad for Ryan. After all, it was his bar mitzvah. And it was he, not Ben-o, who had acknowledged it was *my* choice—to dance or not dance with whoever I wanted to. Yet I hadn't chosen him.

Ben-o was really a terrible dancer. Worse than me, even. We were holding hands in an arm-wrestling pose and were smooshed up too close together. I didn't know where to look. I guessed he was having the same problem, because he was staring over my shoulder in the direction of the dessert table, so I said, just to break the tension, "Are you hungry?"

"What?" he said, sounding confused. "I'm dancing. We're dancing."

"Oh," I said. "I saw you looking at the desserts and I thought . . ." I started sweating then, because I knew I was just babbling, saying anything that popped into my head, and I was desperate to shut up. Ben-o's ears were turning an alarming color, and his eyes were willing me to be quiet, but I rambled on. "Are you thirsty? I mean, I'm not thirsty. I mean, I like dancing with you, and I'm not asking you to stop or anything . . ."

Blah blah blah blah blah. So I guess Ben-o did the one thing he could think of to make me stop talking. He kissed me. A long, drawn-out, mouth-to-mouth kind of kiss, holding my face in both of his hands. That shut me up, all right. But for some reason, I just wanted to cry, right then, just put my head on his shoulder and weep. I didn't even know why. It wasn't that I was unhappy—the opposite. Only not exactly happy, but—it was hard to describe. Relieved. Only not relieved, but maybe a little embarrassed. Because

I hadn't seen it coming. It was like I was someone else, or watching Ben-o kiss someone else—Jenna Alberts, for example. Like I wasn't really there. And all these thoughts felt so STUPID that I suddenly panicked, as if I had said them out loud. Which was impossible, of course, because, like I said, BEN-O WAS KISSING ME. I pulled away to take a deep breath that felt like a gasp and ran outside.

I had on the same gray dress I'd worn to Sheila Rosenberg's bat mitzvah, only I hadn't worn tights this time. It was freezing cold, and I didn't know what I was doing out there. I started to cry for real.

Ben-o came outside then. He didn't say a word, just took off his suit jacket and put it around my shoulders, patting my back like the old Ben-o, the one who hadn't been acting weird lately, who hadn't confessed to Rebecca that he had a crush on me, who hadn't shaved his head just because he thought I wanted him to. Who hadn't just kissed me on the dance floor at Ryan Berger's bar mitzvah. When we went back inside, the deejay was playing a normal song, so Rebecca grabbed my hand and the three of us danced together, and then the moment was over. Like it had never even happened.

This was Ben-o. And me. Best friends since forever. And now—what? He was dancing loosely and avoiding my eyes, which gave me a chance to really look at him, trying to imagine he was someone new, someone who didn't live three floors down, who I hadn't known forever. After all, he *was* one of the cutest boys in our grade. I had been surprised when Jenna said it last year, but now I looked at him—and it was true. Which wasn't the main point, of course, but *still*.

When Rebecca's dad came to pick her up, I told Ben-o I was going with them, just so I didn't have to walk home with him. But I didn't go with them either. I felt like taking a long walk home in the cold. By myself.

Why was I so upset? I knew how he felt about me, but I'd convinced myself he was over it. Over me. That he was interested in Jenna Alberts. It was clear now he was telling her things. As a friend. About us—him and me. *That* made me insanely jealous.

Why couldn't he just come out and tell *me* what he felt? Who was Jenna Alberts to get up in between us? Since when did we need someone else?

Were they best friends now? And if I didn't want to be his girlfriend, if I just wanted us to be BFFs like always—was that position now filled?

It wasn't too long ago that I'd almost lost Rebecca—I'd taken her for granted, and she went and found herself another best friend. That should have woken me up, but it hadn't. Probably I was a very terrible person. Because I had also taken for granted that Ben-o and I would always be friends. Nothing more, nothing less.

I wasn't sure if I could handle such a big change. Almost losing Rebecca made me not want to take chances with Ben-o either. Was it possible to be best friends and boyfriend-girlfriend at the same time? Was that what I wanted? I hadn't been willing to think of him in that way before. Now I couldn't stop.

Chapter 29

I considered faking a headache to get out of Hebrew school on Sunday morning, if only to avoid running into Ben-o downstairs. Then I felt guilty for even thinking that way. Besides, skipping Hebrew school so close to my own bat mitzvah seemed like a bad idea.

Luckily, Ryan Berger took the day off because of his bar mitzvah, so no one gave me a hard time about THE KISS—which I couldn't help thinking about in CAPITAL LETTERS and imagining everyone was gossiping about. I had blown it, big-time.

I invited Sheila to sit next to me in class, on my right. Rebecca sat to my left, pretending to be absorbed in the lesson sheet. Sheila gazed at her mournfully. Since I couldn't concentrate on the lesson and I didn't want to dwell on what had happened with Ben-o, I occupied myself by thinking about my ex-sari bat mitzvah dress, which Gran was bringing over later.

When I reached home, though, Meena Auntie and Vijay were there. I looked at Mum in blank horror. We had to get rid of Meena Auntie, fast, or somehow get word to Gran. Almost immediately, we heard Gran's key in the lock. It was too late.

"Ruthie-jee!" sang Meena Auntie.

"Meen-a-la," Gran replied. "Tara, wait till you see this." She reached into her enormous purse. Mum's eyes grew wide with terror. Gran drew out a parcel wrapped in tissue paper and began to unwrap it.

"Not now, Gran," I said, tilting my head toward Meena Auntie in what I hoped was a meaningful way.

"Isn't that—" Meena Auntie sputtered.

"You'd hardly recognize it!" Gran said, shaking out the folds. "Isn't it something? Tara, go try it on."

Vijay started laughing like an idiot and pointing, slapping his knee. "Tara's in truh-uh-uh-uh-uh-ble, bah-ha-ha-ha-ha-ha!"

Meena Auntie slapped him with her *dupatta*, but he only laughed harder. Then she turned to Mum. "You have allowed this—this desecration?"

"Meena, let me explain—" Mum began.

"Explain? How you have destroyed Daadiji's only good thing?"

"Meena—please. It was an accident."

"You let that child run wild."

That was a little harsh.

Mum stiffened. *"Enough!"* she barked. *"I* am the mother, *nahi*? Her legal guardian. Not you." That finally shut Auntie up for a minute. I didn't want to stay for the rest of their fight, so I went to my room to try on the dress.

Mum and Auntie were still bickering when I came back wearing the sari dress. They turned to look at me.

"Oh, my goodness," Meena Auntie gasped. "It—it's beautiful!"

Vijay sniffed, wiping phony tears from his eyes.

"What did I tell you?" Gran crowed. "Good as new!"

"Not exactly," said Meena.

"What do you mean, not exactly?" Gran said. "Marvin did a beautiful job. You said so yourself."

Mum nodded vigorously. "I couldn't agree more. He did a *lovely* job. She'll get more use out of the dress than a sari."

"Exactly!" Gran agreed.

Meena Auntie showed the flat palm of her hand, just as Nani used to. "That does not change any of the facts."

I walked up and put my arms around her waist, which is something I never do.

"I'm really, really sorry, Auntie," I said into her neck. "This is all my fault." I explained how much I had wanted to wear the sari to my bat mitzvah. I told her how I planned to mention it in my speech, about my great-grandparents fleeing with their small children in that moment when the entire world must have felt upside down. That I would give anything not to have damaged it.

"Burned it," Vijay coughed into his hand. I was pretty sure no one else heard him.

"I wonder if it's too late to find a new deejay," I said over my shoulder. He stopped laughing.

"No fair, cuz!" he cried. "I kept your secret."

"You *knew* about this?" Meena Auntie asked, turning on him. Vijay cringed.

"I wanted to tell you myself, Auntie," I said.

Meena Auntie nodded. I could see she was still angry, but she had decided to blame it on Mum instead of me, just as I'd predicted. "Thank you, Tara," she said. "I'm glad someone in this family has respect for her elders."

Mum sucked her teeth but didn't say anything.

"All's well that ends well," Gran cried, clapping her hands. "Now, that hem is still a little long for you, Tara. Let me get my sewing things." She pulled out a pincushion and tailor's chalk from her enormous purse. I was surprised she didn't have a sewing machine in there, too. "And what was Marvin thinking here?" she said, grabbing a fistful of extra material around my chest. "I'll have to take that in myself." This was too much for Vijay, and he left the room.

"Stay still. Raise your left arm," Gran said. "Other left."

Chapter 30

Ben-o wasn't in the lobby when I came downstairs for school on Monday.

"He left ten minutes ago," Sal said. "He said to tell you he's got chess practice."

That was a lie, of course. The tournament had been in October, and the next one wasn't until the spring.

"Who?" I asked, pretending not to know.

"Who?" Sal echoed. "Your boyfriend, that's who!"

"He's not my boyfriend," I called over my shoulder as I left.

As I was crossing the street, I heard someone calling, "Tara, wait up!" It was Sheila Rosenberg.

"Guess what?" she said, rolling her eyes. "My parents are letting me redecorate my room—no more purple. It's supposed to make me feel 'empowered.'"

"That's cool," I said. "I'd like to feel more empowered. Think you can have your mom talk to my mom?"

"Not a chance." Sheila giggled.

"I'd paint it black if I were you. Just to keep them on their toes."

"Great idea. Maybe I'll get one of those velvet paintings that glow under black lights."

"Careful," I said. "Black lights are actually purple. Don't want to give them the wrong message."

Sheila laughed.

As we were walking, I looked across the street and there was Rebecca, by herself. When she saw who I was with, she put her head down and walked fast, not crossing over to our side. So, to recap: Neither of my best friends was talking to me. Which made me wonder—was Sheila Rosenberg now my only friend in the whole world? Wouldn't *that* be ironic.

"Hey, Sheila," I said, "I'll catch up with you later, okay? I just need to talk to Rebecca—alone. No offense."

"Okay. See you in science, *Tamar*," she said, calling me by my Hebrew name. A private joke.

"Yeah," I said, forcing a smile just to make her feel better. "See you then—*Shoshana*." She laughed.

"Rebecca, wait," I called, bolting across the street. She stopped and waited for me, but she didn't turn around right away. "Are you really mad at me? For walking with Sheila?"

Rebecca bunched her lips, considering the idea. "I guess not," she said.

"Are you still mad at her?"

"A little."

"She's *really* sorry, you know."

"I know," Rebecca said. "I'll get over it."

"Good, because she needs you. A lot more than she needs me." I looked over and saw Sheila walking, alone now, on the other side of the street. Rebecca stopped for a minute, watching her. Then she seemed to have a change of heart.

"Hey, Sheila," she called. "Over here."

Sheila looked up, the picture of hope. Rebecca waved her over.

"Meet you at the corner," Sheila mouthed, pointing. Rebecca smiled and gave her a thumbs-up.

We waited at the corner for the light to change. Sheila sprinted across the street, arriving a little out of breath.

"Hey," she said shyly.

"Hey," Rebecca said, twining her arm through Sheila's. Then we all three walked to school together. I was feeling so good at that moment, I thought nothing could ruin my mood. Not even the fact that Ben-o had left for school without me and lied about it. Not even, as we approached the school, seeing him and Jenna Alberts whispering together on the front steps.

Not even Ryan Berger and Adam Greenspan chanting dumb old school rhymes, like "Tara and Ben-o sitting in a tree, *k-i-s-s-i-n-g!*" I mean, what decade were they living in? On the upside, I guess that meant Ryan was over me, which was a relief. Except it looked like Ben-o was, too.

In science I stared holes into the back of Ben-o's head, but he didn't turn around even once. At lunchtime, I heaped up my tray with beans and rice and was making my way over to our usual table when Jenna Alberts appeared at my side and steered me toward the back of the cafeteria, to an unfamiliar table by the window.

"Sit," she told me, after shooing away a couple of stray sixth-graders. I sat. "Why did you run away from him?"

"I screwed up," I admitted. "And now Ben-o's not even talking to me. I think."

"He's talking to you," Jenna said. "He thinks you're not talking to him."

"Oh," I said, blinking. *Really?*

"So, what was it like?"

"It was like—nothing."

"Nothing?"

"I was in shock."

"He made me smell his breath this morning, and I gotta tell you," she said, fanning the air, "good move!"

"Jenna!"

"Kidding! He smelled like a whole bucket of Binaca, actually."

"He didn't smell like anything on Saturday. Good or bad."

"Well, he's gonna be extra minty for a while, if you know what I mean. So go kiss him again, while it lasts."

Well, I wasn't going to do *that*, but I knew I needed to talk to him. After lunch, I took a deep breath and walked up to him at his locker. I leaned in close and sniffed. Jenna was right: minty.

Ben-o blinked. "What are you doing?"

"Nothing," I said, blushing. "I need to talk to you."

He raised his hands and then dropped them. "Tara—"

"I'm sorry about Ryan's bar mitzvah. I wasn't ready. Listen—" I took a deep breath. I wasn't really sure what I was going to say until I said it. "This week . . . it's going to be a little crazy for me. My bat mitzvah?"

"I know," Ben-o said.

"I was just—can we—maybe—talk, after that?"

"Talk?" he asked cautiously.

"I mean—Ben-o, you're my best friend. I—"

"It's okay. I get it."

"You do?"

"You just want to be friends, right?"

"I don't *know*," I said. I really didn't. There was nothing "just" about being best friends. "Ben-o . . ." I was a little lost. I mean, if there's one thing I learned this year, it's that I'm not sure about anything. But that doesn't mean I don't want to *try*.

"Just a few more days," I said. "I promise. But for now . . . ?"

Ben-o smiled. "For now we're just friends," he said. "Best friends."

"Exactly," I said.

Chapter 31

My cousins arrived from Cincinnati on Thursday. I couldn't believe Aunt Charlotte let them take two whole days off school, but I guess she felt they needed time before my bat mitzvah to recuperate from traveling. It took them almost sixteen hours to get here, because Jonathan kept getting carsick. It would have been only two hours by plane, but Aunt Charlotte is terrified of flying.

"Isn't it nice when the whole *mishpacha*—the whole family—can be together?" Gran said when they finally got here. Mum just sucked her teeth.

Avi had gone all emo-goth since the last time I saw him, about a year ago. He got this kind of fringy haircut that covered his eyes and was too long on the sides. I secretly hated boys like that, but Avi was okay, even if he did wear black eyeliner and have side bangs. Jonathan's hair was frizzier, like mine, so he'd never get away with that look.

Mum and Daddy slept on the pullout in Mum's office

so Aunt Charlotte and Uncle Robert could have their bedroom. The boys stayed with Gran, in Daddy and Uncle Robert's old room.

Friday night, Meena Auntie came over, and she and Mum decorated my arms and feet with *mehndi*, like a bride. Real *mehndi*—not the Sharpie version I doodled on myself sometimes—is this muddy paste made from ground-up dried henna leaves. It goes on thick, like toothpaste, and greenish brown, but after the mud dries and cracks off, you're left with this pretty reddish-orangeish tattoo that can last for like a week. Some people also use it to dye their hair red. I'm pretty sure it's what Aravind Uncle uses on his mustache.

Mum and Meena Auntie applied it to my skin with a piping bag, like you would use to decorate a cake. It had been a long time since I'd seen them hanging out together and getting all giggly, which was kind of nice. Mum drew a Star of David on my left hand, while Meena did intricate paisleys and geometric patterns on my right forearm. Then they switched sides. It was fun getting the royal treatment. It made me feel happy and drowsy.

"Tara is looking like a *rajkumari*," Meena Auntie observed—a princess. Mum smiled.

"She's my princess," she said, kissing me on the forehead.

"Isn't it nice when the whole *mishpacha* comes together?" I asked, imitating Gran. Mum giggled.

"It is indeed," Auntie said, smiling.

* * *

On Saturday morning I woke up at like five A.M., before the alarm clock, even. I was strangely not nervous. I did one last practice speech in front of the mirror while I brushed my teeth, because I had changed a couple of things at the last minute. I would have a printed copy in front of me during my speech, just in case, but I didn't plan to use it. I got dressed, wiggling into my awesome dress. Then I laughed out loud, realizing I had just thought the words "awesome" and "dress" together.

I wasn't very hungry, but I threw on Mum's old bathrobe and went to get a bowl of cereal. Then I turned on the TV and flopped down on the couch to watch cartoons while Mum did my hair.

"Tara, you're not even dressed yet," she said.

"I am, see?" I said, opening the bathrobe. "I just need to put my shoes on."

"Stay still, Tara," Mum said. She was nervous enough for both of us.

Daddy came into the living room, humming, completely dressed except his tie was undone. He put down a cup of coffee for Mum and a hot cocoa for me, kissing each of us on the cheek. "Careful, you'll get my lipstick on you," Mum said. "Tara—don't you spill that cocoa."

"Relax, Rita," Daddy said, giving her arm a squeeze. "It's going to be a great day."

"Ow, Mum! Easy with the curling iron."

Charlotte and Robert emerged from the bedroom fully dressed, as if they'd been sitting up all night on the edge of their bed, in their best clothes.

"Coffee?" Daddy offered.

Robert nodded gratefully.

"Decaf for me, please," Aunt Charlotte said.

"Good plan," Mum muttered.

We heard a key turn in the door, and there was Gran, her hair fresh and crispy. "What, nobody's ready?" she asked by way of greeting.

"Joshua, what's that *shmutz* on your cheek?" Gran asked. It was Mum's Heavenly Hibiscus lipstick. Mum and I both started laughing. Gran spat on a hanky and began scrubbing Daddy's cheek, hard.

"Ow, Ma! If you want to help, do my tie." He got down on his knees so they were the same height, which made everyone laugh, even Aunt Charlotte.

Gran immediately fell to work, *tsk*ing over the thin silk fabric. "How are you supposed to hold a knot in this *shmatta*? Marvin can get you a nice Canali—"

Mum surveyed my hair and decided it was good enough. "Tara, go put your shoes on," she said. "We are leaving in five minutes."

I looked outside. "Look, Mum! It's snowing!"

"*Five* minutes," Mum said. "And find your galoshes."

Rabbi Aron met us in the sanctuary. I walked up to the

bimah and looked out, imagining how the room was going to look a half hour later, when it would be filled with practically everyone I knew. I hoped no one was going to try to make me laugh. I decided I would focus on the left side of the front row, where Mum and Daddy and Gran would be sitting, and try to block out the rest.

Rabbi pulled me aside. He put both hands on my shoulders and looked me square in the eye. "Are we ready, Tara?"

"Let's do this," I said.

"That's my girl," he said, engulfing me in a hug.

More people started to arrive then. I looked at Daddy and he winked. I smiled again at my *desi mishpacha*. Gran had said it takes a *simcha*—a happy event—to bring the whole family together, and she was right. There was Meena Auntie in the second row with Vijay and Aravind Uncle, who both looked awkward wearing *yarmulkes*. Uncle Robert and Aunt Charlotte were next to them. Avi and Jonathan were in the front row, next to Gran. Cousin Marvin was on her other side. Mum was crushing Daddy's hand, looking both proud and terrified.

Later, Rebecca, Avi, and Jonathan were called to open the ark, and then Daddy, Mum, Gran, Marvin, and Uncle Robert were called up for *aliyot*. I made it through the Torah reading and the *haftarah* without making too many mistakes, I think. A few times, I lost the tune, but Rabbi would hum it softly for me and I was right back on track. No one tried to make me laugh, or else I didn't notice.

After that it was time for my "remarks." I was ready. I barely glanced at the printout in front of me.

Good morning, and welcome to my bat mitzvah. I'm really happy you could all be here to share in my spiritual journey. For a long time, I wasn't sure if I was going to go through with it, but here I am. I had some hard choices to make along the way, but I think it was worth it.

As many of you know, I come from a mixed heritage. My father's family have been New York Jews for as long as anyone can remember. My mother's people are Hindus, from India, but she feels it's important that I point out that she converted to Judaism a long time ago, in case you thought she wasn't Jewish, and that maybe I wasn't either.

Mum smiled sheepishly.

Preparing for my bat mitzvah made me have to think about things I'd never thought about before, and maybe didn't want to. But I'm glad I did. For one thing, I had to ask myself what it means to be Jewish, and especially what it means for *me* to be Jewish. When I was younger, I had a very special relationship with my Indian grandparents—my *nani* and *nana*—who unfortunately both passed away a few years ago. I was worried that maybe by having a bat mitzvah, I was somehow forgetting them. But now I know that inspiration can come from many different sources, and that having multicultural experiences can actually make you

stronger and more accepting of different points of view.
Which is a very important thing, since Jews apparently love
to debate. I also think Nanaji would really have liked my
bat mitzvah. Mum says he was a very spiritual person, and
I think I know what she means by that—that he would have
approved, as long as I did it with an open *heart*. And that,
even though I have doubts about some things, it's okay, as
long as I keep an open *mind*.

So—to this week's *parashah*, which is about Joseph
and his many-colored coat. This is totally appropriate
because of a recent experience I had—but I'll get to that
later. Joseph's brothers were jealous because their father,
Jacob, loved him best and gave him a lot of fancy gifts,
including that special multicolored coat (or tunic, or
whatever it was).

I shot a pointed look at Rabbi Aron, who turned his
head away, trying not to smile.

From my study of Vayeishev, I learned that Joseph
was extremely vain and inconsiderate of his brothers'
feelings, like when he told them about two dreams he had
where they had to bow down to him.

Not having siblings of my own, it was at first hard
for me to understand Joseph. I still don't think he was
very considerate of his brothers, but I did try to at least
understand *how* he could act the way he did. Too often, I
think, poor communication with the people closest to us

can lead to terrible misunderstandings. Maybe he could have sugarcoated the part about them worshipping him, or at least toned it down.

Rabbi had helped me with the next part, obviously:

The commentaries teach us that the brothers, including Joseph himself, couldn't imagine a society with multiple leaders, such as the twelve tribes of Israel that would be their descendants. Instead, they thought that only one person could succeed while the others failed, which meant they had to compete instead of cooperate. They didn't realize that they would each become the leader of their own tribe, because they never used their imagination. If they knew that, they might not have pretended to kill Joseph or sold him to the Ishmaelites as a slave. Rabbi called this a "failure of imagination," and I think that's probably the worst kind of failure of all.

But this part was all mine:

So, back to me. Recently, my auntie gave me a beautiful sari that once belonged to my Indian great-grandmother. I had wanted to wear it today in honor of my *nanaji*—my grandfather—to show that I could be both Indian and Jewish at the same time. Like Joseph's coat, it had many colors—pink, red, black, white, green, and gold—just like the dress that I am wearing today.

I did a little curtsy, which made everyone laugh. I stole a glance at Cousin Marvin and he winked. I continued.

> The reason it is now a dress instead of a sari is that I accidentally burned a hole in it, and you can't wear half a sari. I felt terrible about it. At first I was afraid to tell anyone. Not even my mother, and *definitely* not Meena Auntie.
>
> I asked Rabbi Aron what to do, and he said, "Tara, what do you think the right answer is?" From this I learned that not only does a Jew answer a question with another question, but that it was time for me to take responsibility for my actions, like an adult. This is how I knew I was ready to be a bat mitzvah.
>
> Actually turning the sari into a dress was my gran's idea. I couldn't envision it myself, until she said it, and then I was able to see the possibilities. I don't mean to say that my dress is as important as the twelve tribes of Israel, but I think you get my point. All I needed was a little imagination.

"Sorry, Auntie," I added, looking up. Meena Auntie smiled.

I turned to the end of my printed speech and realized the last page—with the list of people I wanted to thank—was missing. I was going to have to wing it.

"I'd like to thank Gran for teaching me an important lesson: When life gives you lemons, make lemonade. And when life gives you a sari with a big hole in it, make a new dress."

Everyone laughed again. Gran reached over and pinched Marvin's cheek.

"And thank you, Cousin Marvin, for making this beautiful dress. Oh, and thanks, Mum and Daddy and Rabbi Aron, for everything else . . . Amen," I added. I stood there, uncertain if I'd forgotten something important, but Rabbi Aron was beaming.

"Thank *you*, Tara, for that . . . very original interpretation of scripture," he said. He went on to tell the congregation how impressed he had been by my many thought-provoking questions these last few months and said that not everyone my age is mature enough to know what they don't know. Which was a nice way of putting it.

Rabbi said my mastery of dialectic reasoning was nothing short of Talmudic, and if I still didn't know what that meant, I should look it up. He also said I had a bright career ahead of me as a lawyer or a philosopher. Everyone laughed at that, especially Meena Auntie.

✳ ✳ ✳

Well, like I said, this bat mitzvah thing wasn't my idea originally, but I'm glad I did it. I still don't know if I believe in God, but on the other hand—I don't *not* believe in God, either. And Rabbi had said it's okay not to know.

At the reception, I danced with Ben-o (twice), then Rebecca led the whole dance floor in an old-school Electric Slide. I sat down to take a breath just as Vijay started playing a *hora*. Daddy and Uncle Robert hoisted me up above their heads, chair and all. Then they tried to get Gran to sit in the chair, and she wouldn't. So they linked hands to form a swing and scooped her off her feet, dancing wildly. She screamed and clung to their necks. When they came for Mum, she ran and hid in the ladies' room.

Vijay's deejaying was actually pretty amazing. He slid so easily from the *hora* to a *bhangra*/hip-hop mix that even Aunt Charlotte had no choice but to join in. Which was pretty hilarious. And he only played "Billie Jean" once, because my great-aunt Tilly asked him to and he couldn't say no. When I caught his eye, he shrugged so helplessly that I just laughed and kept dancing. Ryan Berger and Adam Greenspan had liberated a bottle of kosher wine from the *kiddush* and spent the afternoon puking in the boys' bathroom. When it came time to light candles, I saw Mum slide an arm under Gran's elbow to steady her. Gran patted her on the cheek and smiled. The hall was festooned with long garlands of marigolds, which Mum had arranged as a special surprise for me. Aunt Charlotte and Jonathan couldn't stop sneezing the whole time.

Aravind Uncle stood outside most of the afternoon, ruminating on a wad of *paan*. He looked small inside an enormous muffler wound six times around his head, his breath forming puffs of steam in the frigid December air. I saw Meena Auntie go outside and scold him for standing in the cold, her hands gesturing wildly. A branch gave way overhead, showering them with fresh snow. They both laughed. Meena Auntie reached down with her bare hands and scooped up a pile of snow, which she smooshed in Uncle's face. He sputtered and looked shocked, but then he reached down for a fistful of his own and poured it down Auntie's back. I saw her gasp from the cold, but then she started to laugh—and laugh and laugh. She turned and kissed him on the cheek, and he smiled and took her hand, and they came back inside and danced awkwardly together.

Sheila wore a short, floaty, red—as in, not purple—dress that Mum said looked "stunning" with her hair and eyes. I had to admit she looked great. I noticed she wasn't wearing the crystal bracelet.

Across the room, Ben-o was telling something to Jenna Alberts and Aisha Khan. Jenna gave him a pat on the back and he blushed. We locked eyes and he smiled.

Daddy gave my arm a gentle squeeze. "See—what did I tell you? It's a great day, isn't it?"

It was a great day.

✳ ✳ ✳

Afterward, Rebecca and Sheila came over and we ate leftover bat mitzvah cake while I opened some of my presents. Sheila's was a beautiful gold necklace with my name and a Star of David: *Tara* ✡. I'm not even sure if she knew how exactly appropriate that was. *Tara* does mean "star" in Hindi, after all. I lifted my hair and she helped me put it on.

There was a handmade card from Rebecca. The Goldsteins had already given me my gift the day before, a pair of dangly gold earrings with my birthstone—blue topaz. I'd been wearing them all day, enjoying the soft jingly sound whenever I moved my head. I shook the envelope, not expecting anything else to be inside, but I could hear something rattling.

"Uh-oh," I said. "Is it broken?" Rebecca shook her head, smiling. When I opened the envelope to pull out the card, grains of colored rice sprayed everywhere. On the front of the card, she had drawn a picture of Ganesha wearing a *tallit*—prayer shawl—and holding a Jewish prayer book.

"**Have a very . . .**" it said below that, in perfect calligraphy.

And inside:

> **. . . Basmati Bat Mitzvah!!!**
> **Best friends forever,**
> **Rebecca**

She bit her lip nervously. "Do you like it?"

"I love it!" I said, throwing the rice at her.

I glanced over at the remaining pile of gifts—mostly envelopes, but a few boxes as well. Ben-o's gift was in there somewhere.

"Hey," I told Sheila and Rebecca, "I'm kind of beat . . ."

"Okay," Rebecca said. "Want us to come over tomorrow and open the rest?"

"That's okay," I said. "They're probably all savings bonds from Gran's relatives."

"Yeah." Sheila laughed. "I got a lot of those, too."

After they left, I found Ben-o's gift. He had obviously wrapped it himself, in layers of brown paper, aluminum foil, and comics, held together with duct tape. There was a smaller box taped to the top, like a robot's head.

I put the Frankenstein-ish thing on my bed and studied it. It was definitely supposed to be a robot. I worked at the layers of duct tape with a pair of scissors. I smiled, imagining the evil grin on his face as he had wrapped it. The smaller box was marked *Open Me First*. So I opened the bigger one instead.

Inside was a pile of parts that I recognized as his mom's old Roomba, plus a brand-new set of triangle-head screwdrivers. I laughed and reached for the smaller box.

It turned out to be the best present of all—a Bluetooth robot interface module. Which was extra nice of him, since I was still his main competition for the finals. And he had probably saved up for it on his own.

I had to laugh. Somehow he had nailed it, knowing I would be more psyched by this present than something

silly and romantic, like flowers or jewelry. He knew me that
well. Like a best friend should. A best friend who might also
be my boyfriend soon. It didn't have to be weird or different; it would just be us.

I stood in front of the bathroom mirror and brushed out
the curling-iron curls, so I just looked like me again, which
was reassuring. I had promised Ben-o we'd talk after my bat
mitzvah. So what if it had only been a few hours? I was ready
now. And what I'd decided was . . . yes. If he still wanted to,
yes. I was willing to try.

"Let's do this," I told my reflection.

✳ ✳ ✳

I changed into sweats and went downstairs to Ben-o's,
bringing a plate of leftover cake and a DVD. I knocked on the
door with my bare foot. Mrs. O opened the door, with baby
Nina on her hip.

"Tara! Big day for you," said Mrs. O.

"Tata!" Nina echoed.

"Yeah," I said. "I brought some cake."

"What's that thing you say? Matzoh top?"

"It's *mazel tov*," I said. "And thanks."

Mrs. O laughed. "Benjy, Tara's here," she called.

"Hey," Ben-o said.

"Hey," I said.

We went into the kitchen and made two bags of microwave popcorn, while Ben-o ate the leftover cake.

"Behind the graham crackers," he said, between mouthfuls, as I rummaged through the cabinet over the sink. There it was—my emergency jar of *chaat masala*. I sprinkled some over my bag of popcorn, and then we went to the living room.

"What are we watching?" he asked.

"You'll see," I said, popping in the DVD.

"Oh, no." He groaned as the Indian music started up. "Not this again."

"What? You haven't seen this one."

"But they're all the same," he said.

"Don't be racist."

I flopped down on the couch. Ben-o sat on the floor, with his head resting next to me. His hair was starting to grow back, but more outward than downward. It made his head look enormous, but at least it put the sippy-cup ears in proportion.

I reached over and ran my hands through his hair, smoothing it down.

"What are you doing?"

"Nothing," I said. "Just reminding myself what your head looks like without that poufy hair."

"I have a surprise for you," he said, moving to sit next to me on the couch. "I've been waiting all day to tell you."

"What is it?"

"Adam's and Ryan's probation is up. Know what that means?" He didn't wait for me to answer. "They're dropping out of Robotics!"

"They are? Ryan didn't tell me that."

Ben-o tactfully ignored that comment. "Anyway, that leaves both of us without partners, and Mr. H said—I mean, if you still want to . . ."

Of course I wanted to. But there was something more important on my mind. And it was now or never. So I did the one thing I could think of to make him stop talking about Robotics. I leaned in and gave him a kiss. Not a long, drawn-out, mouth-to-mouth kind of kiss, but a kiss just the same. On the cheek. I smiled at my own *chutzpah*.

Ben-o put his thumb under my chin and moved my head so we were eye to eye. I had nowhere to look but right back at him. At first I was terrified I was going to start babbling again, like I did at Ryan Berger's bar mitzvah, so instead I closed my eyes and took a deep breath. It was going to be okay. Change was good, right? Ben-o leaned in and kissed me. Right on the lips. This time I didn't pull away, or freak out. I just let my lips linger next to his. All the awkwardness melted away. The urge to babble passed, and I just stayed there, breathing in his sweet, minty, salty, cake-filled breath.

I opened my eyes.

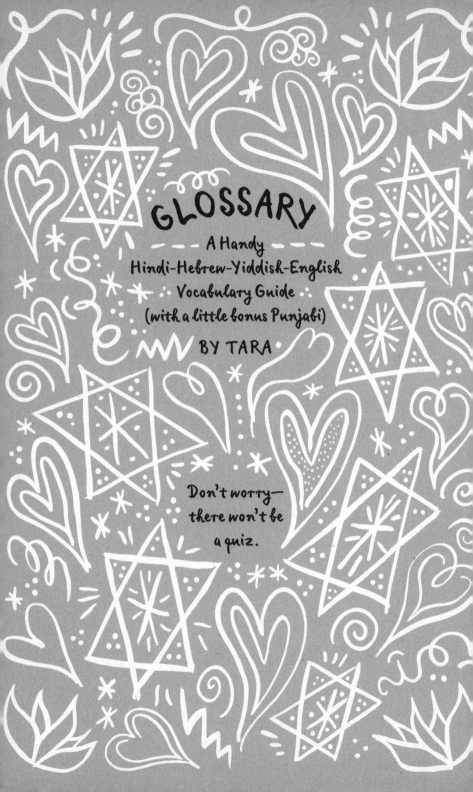

GLOSSARY

--- A Handy ---
Hindi-Hebrew-Yiddish-English
Vocabulary Guide
(with a little bonus Punjabi)

BY TARA

Don't worry—
there won't be
a quiz.

ach-cha! HINDI (ah-CHAH, like *"ah-CHOO!"*) All-purpose exclamation meaning "Okay," "All right," "Oh," "Ah," "Aha!" "Is that so?" "Really?" "I see." See, what did I tell you? All-purpose.

aliyah HEBREW (ah-LEE-ya) Being called to read from the Torah. Also means the immigration of Jews to Israel.

aloo HINDI ("Ah, Lou.") Potato

alter kocker YIDDISH (OLL-ter kocker) "Old fart" is close enough.

arrey HINDI (Sounds like *array*.) Hey or "My goodness!" Equivalent to Yiddish "Oy!" or English "Seriously?"

Ashkenazi/ Ashkenazim YIDDISH (ahsh-kuh-NAH-zee/ahsh-kuh-NAH-zim) Jewish person/people from parts of central and eastern Europe. *Yiddish* is the language they developed. See also *Sephardic*.

bar mitzvah HEBREW (bar MITS-vuh) Jewish coming-of-age ceremony for boys, usually held at age thirteen, after which they're supposed to be treated as adults. As if.

bat mitzvah or bas mitzvah HEBREW/YIDDISH (baht MITS-vuh/bahs MITS-vuh) Jewish coming-of-age ceremony for girls, usually held at age twelve or thirteen. Because girls are much more mature than boys, obvs.

basmati HINDI (BAHS-mah-tee) The most delicious and best-smelling rice. It has a long grain and is never sticky or lumpy. It would be almost impossible to eat it with chopsticks.

Bereishit HEBREW "In the Beginning." The first chapter of the Torah, about the creation of the universe. For the record, it's pronounced "buh-RAY-sheet."

beta HINDI (BAY-tah) Literally means "son," but it's an extra-cute thing to call a girl. See *bubeleh*.

bhangra	PUNJABI (BHAHN-gruh. There's no English equivalent of the Hindi *bh-* sound. You can get away with saying something halfway between a *b* and a *p*.) High-energy folk music and dance often blended with Western pop.
bhel puri	HINDI (That *b/p* sound again: BHAYL POOR-ee.) An addictive little snack made from puffed rice, little fried noodles, and lentils, usually mixed with vegetables, onions, and tamarind chutney. It's a lot better than it sounds.
"Billie Jean"	A vintage pop song by Michael Jackson that Indians love for some reason. It's been played at every Indian celebration I've ever been to, including weddings, sweet sixteens, and cultural events.
bimah	HEBREW (BEE-muh) In a synagogue, the podium or platform where the Torah is read.
bindi	HINDI (BIN-dee) A decorative mark on the forehead, usually shaped like a dot. Traditionally drawn with vermillion powder or paste, but now there are stick-on ones made from velvet and crystal and stuff.
Bollywood	HINGLISH The biggest film industry in the world is in Bombay (Mumbai), not Hollywood. Seriously.
bubeleh	YIDDISH (BUHB-el-uh) "Little grandma" (which in Gran's case is redundant), but it's just a sweet thing to call someone, even if the person's a boy. See *beta*.
chaat	HINDI (CHAH-t) Munchies or snack food. *Chaat masala* is the mix of spices typically used on them.
chaiwallah	HINDI (*ch-* like in *cheese*. CHY-wah-luh) Someone who sells tea (*chai*). See *-wallah*.
chalo	HINDI (CHUH-lo) "Let's go." "Vamanos." "Skiddoo."
chana	HINDI (CHUHN-uh) Chickpea.

chutzpah	YIDDISH (The *ch-* here sounds more like a very hard *h* or *kh*. My best advice is to clear your throat while saying it: HUT-spuh, or KHUT-spuh.) Nerve, hubris, spirit, arrogance, guts. As the great Leo Rosten puts it in *The Joys of Yiddish*, chutzpah is "that quality enshrined in a man who, having killed his mother and father, throws himself on the mercy of the court because he is an orphan."
daadi/ daadiji	HINDI (DAH-dee/DAH-dee-jee) Grandmother (specifically, your father's mother). See *-ji*.
desi	HINDI/HINGLISH (DAY-see) How Indians outside of India refer to each other. Pronounced "DAY-see," not "Dezzy" like Desi Arnaz. Literally means "of a country"—native, countryman, compadre, brother, amigo. Like that.
desi mishpacha	HINDI + YIDDISH (DAY-see mish-PA-kuh) Made-up term meaning a family that's a little bit Indian and a little bit Jewish. Nicer than "Hin-Jew," I think.
dhol	HINDI (Sounds like *dole* but with a softer *d*, like in *duh*.) Type of drum typically used in *bhangra* music.
dudhwallah	HINDI (DOOD-wah-luh, with that soft *d* again.) Milkman. See *-wallah*.
Diwali	HINDI (dee-WAH-lee or dee-VAH-lee) Festival of Lights. See *Hanukkah*.
Diwalikkah	HINDI + HEBREW (dee-WAH-lee-kuh) A made-up word for when *Diwali* and *Hanukkah* happen close together.
dupatta	HINDI (doo-PUH-tuh) Scarf.
fruitwallah	HINGLISH (FROOT-wah-luh) Someone who sells fruit. See *-wallah*.
Ganesha	(ga-NAY-shuh or ga-NAYSH) One of the major Hindu gods. Ganesha is the son of Shiva and

Parvati, recognizable because he has the head of an elephant. In one explanation, Parvati created a boy to stand guard outside while she took a bath. When Shiva returned home, the strange child refused to let him in. In a rage, Shiva beheaded him, which made Parvati sad and angry. So Shiva promised to bring the boy back to life by giving him the head of the first creature he could find, which happened to be an elephant.

golgappa   HINDI (gol-GUH-puh) A crispy little round pastry shell filled with water, tamarind, onions, chickpeas, and spices. Also called *panipuri*—*pani* (water) + *puri* (deep-fried bread).

goy/goyim   YIDDISH (SINGULAR/PLURAL) (GOY/GOY-im) Anyone who is not Jewish. Which, of course, is almost everyone. Warning: relatively rude. A sentence or phrase starting with "The *goyim* . . ." usually leads into a prejudicial statement or ridiculous generalization.

haan   HINDI (HAHN) Yes.

haftarah   HEBREW (haf-TAH-ruh, sometimes haf-TOH-ruh) A chapter from the Prophets, read after the weekly Torah portion. One of the most important duties of a *bar mitzvah* or *bat mitzvah*. *Haftorah* in Yiddish.

Hanukkah   HEBREW (HAH-nuh-kuh or KHA-nuh-kuh) Festival of Lights. See *Diwali*.

Hinglish   A word or phrase that's part Hindi, part English. "Hinglish" itself is a Hinglish word.

Hin-Jew   HINGLISH Someone who is Indian and Jewish or who grew up among both communities. Depending on who says it and how they say it, can be either endearing or rude. Ryan Berger thinks he invented it, but he's not that smart.

hora   HEBREW (HOH-ruh or HOOR-uh) A festive circle dance. If you've ever been to a bar mitzvah, you know.

-ji or -jee	HINDI ("Gee!") Respectful suffix. See *nanaji, naniji, mataji*. Can be attached to a person's name, like when Meena Auntie calls Gran "Ruthie-jee."
kiddush	HEBREW (KID-ish or ki-DOOSH) Ritual following Shabbat morning services, in which a blessing is said over wine or bread.
kratsn	YIDDISH (KRAWT-sin) To scratch.
kulfi	HINDI (*kul-* rhymes with *bull*: KUL-fee.) Like ice cream, but better. Because it's made with condensed milk.
latke	YIDDISH (LAHT-kuh) Means just "pancake," but when people talk about latkes, they almost always mean *potato* latkes. See *tikki*.
masala	HINDI (mah-SAH-lah) Spice or mix of spices.
mata/mataji	HINDI (MAH-tah/MAH-tah-jee) Mother. *Mataji* (respectful form) is what Vijay calls Meena Auntie when he's being disrespectful. See *-ji*.
matzoh/ matzoh ball	HEBREW/YINGLISH (MAHT-suh; rhymes with *lotsa*.) Matzoh is a cracker-ish flat bread eaten on Passover. It doesn't taste like anything, except maybe cardboard (I've never eaten cardboard, so this is a guess). Matzoh balls are dumplings made from ground matzoh meal and usually served in chicken soup. Light, fluffy, and delicious, they taste nothing at all like boring old flat matzoh. Everyone thinks their grandmother's matzoh ball soup is the best, but that's only because they've never tasted Gran's. The trick is to get them to be light and fluffy while maintaining structural integrity—not so hard that you can play golf with them, not so soft that they fall apart in the soup. It's a delicate balance that takes about fifty years of experience to get right.
mazel tov	HEBREW AND YIDDISH (MAH-zul tohv) Congratulations.

mehndi	HINDI (MEN-dee) Henna, a plant used to make hair dye and temporary tattoos—which are traditional for special occasions, especially weddings, or just for fun.
menorah	HEBREW (muh-NOOR-uh) Candleholder used in Jewish worship.
meshugge	YIDDISH (-*shugge* sounds a lot like *sugar* without the *r*: muh-SHOOG-uh.) Crazy. Nuts. Full of *mishegoss*.
meshuggener or **meshuggeneh**	YIDDISH (MASCULINE/FEMININE) (muh-SHOOG-uh-ner/muh-SHOOG-uh-nuh) Person who is *meshugge*.
mezuzah	HEBREW (me-ZOO-zuh) Tiny scroll containing a handwritten verse from the Torah, enclosed in a little case and attached to the doorpost of your house or apartment.
mishegoss	YIDDISH (MISH-uh-gahs) Craziness, mayhem.
mishpacha	HEBREW (mish-PA-kuh) Family, clan.
Mishpatim	HEBREW (mish-pa-TEEM) Judgments or laws. The chapter of the Torah that's about Jewish laws. I love that "*mishegoss*" and "Mishpatim" sound almost the same.
Mumbai	(moom-BYE or MOOM-bye) The largest city in India (formerly called Bombay in English, which is where the word *Bollywood* comes from).
naches	YIDDISH (The *ch* is pronounced like a *k*: NAHK-ess, not *nachos*.) Pride, joy. You're always giving your grandmother either *naches* or *tsuris*.
nafka	YIDDISH (You don't need to know how to pronounce this.) Never call anyone this. Just don't.

nahi
or nahee   HINDI (Pronounce it with a barely perceptible *n* at the end: NUH-hee[n] or nuh-HEE[n].) No.

nana/nanaji   HINDI (NAH-nuh/NAH-nuh-gee) Grandfather (specifically, your mother's father). Does not mean grand-mother, like it does in English. That's why Gran is called "Gran" and not "Nana." See -*ji*.

nani/naniji   HINDI (NAH-nee/NAH-nee-gee) Grandmother; specifically, your mother's mother. Not to be confused with *nana*, which means grandfather. See -*ji*.

no-goodnik   YINGLISH Exactly what it sounds like.

om   HINDI (OHm) A Sanskrit syllable that is a common symbol of Hindu philosophy. It looks like this: ॐ

paan   HINDI (PAHn) Breath freshener made from a betel leaf stuffed with assorted fillings like betel nuts, lime, rose-petal jam, fennel seeds, and coconut. People chew it like tobacco or gum. You can tell if someone is a *paan* chewer because it stains their teeth red.

parashah   HEBREW (PAR-uh-shah or PAR-shah) Chapter from the Torah.

pataka   HINDI (pa-TAH-kuh) Firecracker. It's an onomatopoeia (look it up).

pullao   HINDI (pull-AU) A kind of side dish of basmati rice. Same thing as pilaf.

rajkumari   HINDI (raj-coo-MAR-ee) Princess.

Raksha
Bandhan
or Rakhi   HINDI (RAHK-shah BUN-dhun/RAHK-hee) "Bond of Protection." Festival celebrating the relationship between brothers and sisters, or boy—girl cousins. The bracelet that girls give their brothers that day is also called a *rakhi*.

salwar kameez	HINDI (sal-WAHR [or sal-VAHR] ka-MEEZ) *Salwar* is pants. *Kameez* is shirt (like *camisa* in Spanish). A kind of loose Indian-style pantsuit.
sari	HINDI (SAH-ree) A looooooooong piece of fabric that is wrapped, folded, and tucked in to form a traditional garment for women. Typically done without pins or other security measures, if you know what you're doing.
Sephardim	HEBREW (suh-FAR-dim) Sephardim (or Sephardic Jews) are Jewish people from Spain, Portugal, and parts of Asia, the Middle East, and North Africa. See also *Ashkenazi*.
Shabbat or Shabbos	HEBREW/YIDDISH (sha-BAHT/SHA-bus) The Jewish holy day, the Sabbath, a.k.a. day of rest.
shiksa	YIDDISH (SHIK-suh) Non-Jewish girl or woman. Warning: rude. See *goyim*.
shmatta	YIDDISH (SHMA-tuh) Rag. Rhymes with *dupatta*. Coincidence?
shmear	YIDDISH (SHMEER) Smudge, smear; to spread (like cream cheese).
shmutz	YIDDISH (SHMUUTS) Dirt. Unbelievably, this word is not in *The Joys of Yiddish*.
shomer Shabbos	YIDDISH (SHOH-mer SHA-bus) Person who observes *Shabbat* pretty seriously.
simcha	YIDDISH (SIM-kuh) Happy occasion, celebration, event.
tallit or tallis	HEBREW/YIDDISH (tah-LIT/TAHL-es) Prayer shawl.
Talmud	HEBREW (TAHL-mood) A massive collection of commentaries, interpretations, and debates on the Torah, biblical law, ethics, traditions, etc., compiled over more than one thousand years (!!!).

tara or **taara**	HINDI (TAH-ruh) Star. Like me! ✿
teeka	HINDI (TEE-kuh) A religious mark made from powder or paste, usually on the forehead.
tikki	HINDI (TICK-ee) Patty or croquette. *Aloo tikki* and potato *latkes* are practically the same thing.
tsuris	YIDDISH (TSOO-ris) Troubles, aggravation.
tuchis	YIDDISH (TOOKH-is) Rear end, butt. Again, the *ch* is pronounced like a *k*, but harder, as if you had to clear your throat.
Vayeishev	HEBREW (va-YAY-shev) "And he lived." The chapter of the Torah that's about Joseph.
-wallah	HINDI (WAH-luh) Suffix that basically means "one" or "person who . . ." So a *dudhwallah* is one who sells *dudh* (milk), a *kulfiwallah* makes *kulfi*, etc. Handily, you can attach it to almost any noun, in any language: *chaiwallah, fruitwallah, computerwallah, mishegoss-wallah*. Similar to *-nik*, as in *no-goodnik* (no-good-wallah?).
yarmulke	YIDDISH (YA-muh-kuh or YAR-muh-kuh) Head covering worn by many Jews during prayer—or all the time, depending on how religious they are. Usually the wearers are men, but a few women wear them, too. The Hebrew word is *kippah*.
yenta	YIDDISH (YEN-tuh) Super-inquisitive, nosy person; gossip queen. See *Gran* (jk!).
LAST BUT NOT LEAST . . . **Yiddish**	YIDDISH Informal language of Ashkenazi Jews of Europe and their descendants. Literally means "Jewish"—but meaning language, not person. Its vocabulary is mostly from German and some Hebrew, with a sprinkling of other European languages, including, more recently, English. Yiddish is an exceptionally great source of insults and funny expressions.

Acknowledgments

Some of my favorite kids, little and big, inspired me to write this book, albeit indirectly. Daydreaming about any one of them enjoying it motivated me to get it done. I thank, alphabetically, David, Eliana, Mana, Rachel, Samantha, and Stacie.

I thank the many who were roped into reading the manuscript at various stages; your praises uplifted me, and your criticisms of early drafts made the end result much better than it had any right to be. Thank you, Kulbir Arora, Laura Freedman, Norma Freedman, Kim B., Margaret Crocker, Stacey Goldsmith Nathanson, Faith Childs, Sharon Reiss Baker, Wendy Brandes, Jessica Benjamin, and the late Deborah Brodie—to name only a few.

I get my love of language, from crossword puzzles to Yiddishisms, from my late father, Howard Freedman, and I acquired a secondhand taste for trilingual punning from my husband, Kulbir, with whom I have spent exactly half my life so far (the better half).

A few specifics:

For proper Yiddish usage (if that's a thing), I consulted

the good book—*The Joys of Yiddish*, by Leo Rosten. I was especially thankful for the Kindle edition, so that I didn't have to schlep the hardcover—which weighs more than my laptop—all over the city.

Margaret Crocker made sure I actually wrote on our writing dates.

Deborah Brodie, may she rest in peace, encouraged me at every step. When I lost the plot, had writer's block, or fell too madly in love with my own words, I reminded myself that Deborah would not have tolerated such self-indulgence, and I got back on track.

Kathy Sharpe, among a thousand other demonstrations of friendship, introduced me to my fearless agent, Judith Riven. I am indebted to both of them. Thank you, Judith, for discerning the potential in this book (and me) well before I did.

Kim B. helped me maintain my sanity throughout.

I am grateful to Susan Van Metre and Erica Finkel for their fine editorial vision, and everyone behind the scenes at Amulet for believing in this project.

Special thanks to Shivani Desai, who has grace and maturity beyond her years.

Finally, and somewhat redundantly, to my *desi mishpacha*—to my family on both sides, on two continents. Mom and Dad; my sisters, Julia, Laura, and Janet; Kulbir (again and always); Mana; Pammi Didi; and Janam Bhaisaheb, for their patience, humor, support, and love in this and all things. Thank you.

AUTHOR'S NOTE

...·|·...

Even though I'm generally
more of an eater than a cook,
writing this book inspired me
to try out some recipes that
combine my Jewish roots and
my husband's Indian roots.

Here are some
recipes that give
a nod to both.

Matzoh Balls in Sambhar

Sambhar is a traditional South Indian soup made from toor daal (split pigeon peas). It's often served with idli (fermented rice dumplings), which look sort of like matzoh balls, only flatter. That was the idea behind this mash-up.

The matzoh balls are my mother's recipe—except for the turmeric, of course. The ingredients are simple, but you must understand that ninety percent of the success of a matzoh ball lies in the technique. My mom has been doing it flawlessly for about thirty-five years, so don't feel bad if yours aren't perfectly round or if they fail to exhibit the magical balance of density and fluffiness. It takes years of practice. If they don't fall apart in the soup, you've already passed a major life milestone.

Both the matzoh balls and the sambhar can be made a couple of days in advance

Note: You may think your mom's/grandma's recipe is somehow better than this one, and that's a nice illusion for you to cherish. Feel free to substitute, but, really, this recipe is best.

For the matzoh balls

4 extra-large eggs

6 ounces cold seltzer

½ teaspoon salt

dash of pepper

1 cup matzoh meal

optional: 2 teaspoons ground turmeric (for a bit of desi color)

Beat first four ingredients. Add matzoh meal and turmeric and beat some more.

Cover and refrigerate mixture for at least 4 hours or overnight.

In a large pot, boil salted water. Oil hands and shape mixture into balls, each about the size of a large meatball. Drop into boiling water. Keep oiling hands as necessary. (It's easiest to put some oil on a saucer and dip your fingers in that.)

Add any leftover oil to the pot. Cover with lid slightly ajar. Lower heat to medium and cook about 35–40 minutes.

Gently remove matzoh balls from water with a slotted spoon. Place in large bowl or container, add some of the cooking water, cover, and refrigerate.

Makes about 12 matzoh balls.

For the sambhar

2 cups dried split pigeon peas (toor daal), rinsed/presoaked (or not, according to package directions)

6 cups water

1 tablespoon salt

3 cups chopped vegetables (such as fresh carrots,
   zucchini, string beans, cooked potatoes)

1 cup chopped onions

2 medium tomatoes

1 heaping tablespoon tamarind paste

Dry spices (amount shown or to taste)

1 tablespoon ground cumin

1 tablespoon ground coriander

1/2 teaspoon black pepper

1/4 teaspoon cayenne pepper

1 teaspoon ground turmeric

For tempering ("tadka")

1 tablespoon oil

2 whole dried chili peppers

1 tablespoon black mustard seeds

1 teaspoon fenugreek seeds

1/4 cup fresh whole curry leaves

Place split peas, water, and salt in a large pot. Bring to a boil, partially cover, and reduce heat to simmer for about 35 minutes. Mash or blend the lentils until smooth. Add 2–4 more cups of water until soup is fairly thin.

Add vegetables, onions, tomatoes, and tamarind paste to the soup, stir, and cook covered for 20 minutes or until tender. Add dry spices and more salt to taste. Turn off heat.

In a small frying pan, heat the oil. When very hot, add the chili peppers, mustard seeds, fenugreek seeds, and curry leaves. Flash-fry for about a minute (or less if mustard seeds start to pop). Pour mixture on top of the soup, letting it sizzle. Stir when it stops sizzling.

You can refrigerate the sambhar for a day to incorporate all the flavors.

When ready to serve, reheat the sambhar. Drain off water from the matzoh balls and add the matzoh balls to the sambhar. Cook until warmed through. Serve.

Aloo Latkes Chaat

*a*s you know by now, potato latkes and aloo tikki are similar (both are types of potato pancakes), but they're prepared differently. This recipe does it latkes style, but spiced up and served tikki style, with chutneys and yogurt on top.

3–4 medium potatoes, peeled and shredded

1 small onion, finely chopped

1 egg

2 tablespoons matzoh meal or flour

1 teaspoon coarse salt

black pepper to taste

½ teaspoon ground ginger powder

½ teaspoon ground cumin powder

½ teaspoon ground coriander powder

dash of cayenne pepper

oil for frying

Toppings

sweet tamarind chutney

green chutney (coriander or mint)
plain yogurt, stirred, with a pinch of salt added
pinch of chaat masala powder

Place grated potatoes and onions in a strainer over a medium bowl, squeezing out as much liquid as possible. (This will make them fry up extra crispy.) Transfer potatoes and onions from the strainer to another bowl.

Carefully drain the potato liquid out of the first bowl. See that white powdery stuff at the bottom? That's lovely potato starch! Scrape it out and add it to the potatoes. Add the eggs, matzoh meal, salt, and dry spices; mix well.

Heat a large fry pan on medium-high. Add just enough oil to completely cover the bottom of the pan. Form the potato mixture into balls and drop them into the hot oil, one at time. Use a spatula to flatten them into patties.

Note: After flattening the latkes, you're probably going to want to keep pressing down on them while they cook. Don't. Nothing good will come of it. This is also true of hamburgers, by the way. Put down that spatula until it's time to flip the latkes.

Cook latkes until underside is golden brown. Flip latkes over and cook the other side. Transfer to a paper-towel-covered plate to absorb excess oil.

To serve, arrange latkes on a plate. Swirl a teaspoon of tamarind, green chutney, and yogurt over each latke. Top with a pinch of our good friend, chaat masala.

Pistachio or Fennel Seed Mandel Toast

Mandel toast is basically Jewish biscotti. The following is based on my mom's recipe, which she got from her aunt Betty. "Mandel" literally means "almond," but we've switched the flavors here to give it an Indian twist.

3 eggs

1 cup sugar

1 cup oil

3½ cups sifted flour

2 teaspoons baking powder

dash of salt

1 teaspoon vanilla or almond extract

¼ teaspoon ground cardamom

¼ teaspoon ground cinnamon

⅛ teaspoon ground cloves

1 cup shelled pistachios, roughly chopped, or 2 tablespoons plain fennel seeds (to mix in) and 1 tablespoon candy-coated fennel seeds (to sprinkle on top)

Beat eggs. Add sugar and oil and beat well.

Sift together flour, baking powder, and salt. Add to egg mixture and beat. Add the vanilla or almond extract.

Mix pistachios or plain fennel seeds into the dough (or divide the dough and put ½ cup pistachios in one and 1 tablespoon plain fennel seeds in the other).

Oil two cookie sheets. Divide dough and shape into four long rectangular loaves, about 1 inch thick. Sprinkle candied fennel seeds over the fennel loaf.

Bake at 300 degrees for ½ hour. Remove the loaves from the oven and slice while hot, separating the slices a little. Return to oven and bake for 10 minutes more. Then turn off heat and leave in oven for 2–3 hours, until crunchy.

Mango-Ginger Hamantaschen

Hamantaschen are triangles of deliciousness traditionally eaten on Purim or anytime you crave a marvelous filled cookie or pastry. Haman was the villain of the Purim story. I grew up believing "tasch" meant "hat" (so "Haman's hat," because he allegedly wore a three-cornered one). But like so many things I think I remember from my youth, that turns out not to be true. "Tasch" really means "pocket." ("Haman's pocket"? Whatever.) I don't know what's real anymore.

For the dough

3 eggs

1¼ cups sugar

1 cup oil

1 teaspoon vanilla extract

1 teaspoon salt

½ cup orange juice

1 tablespoon baking powder

5½ cups flour

For the filling

1 can (16 ounces) sliced mangoes in light syrup

1 whole star anise

dash of salt

2 tablespoons sugar or more to taste

½ teaspoon ground ginger powder

Make the dough

Beat eggs, oil, vanilla, and orange juice in a large bowl. Sift together sugar, salt, baking powder, and flour, and add to the egg mixture. Mix well. Set aside or cover and refrigerate.

Make the filling

Drain the mangoes, reserving the syrup. Place mangoes and remaining ingredients in a saucepan. Cover and simmer on low heat for 10 minutes. Uncover and mash the cooked fruit. Add the syrup. Stir well. Cook uncovered on low heat, stirring frequently, until mixture reaches a jellylike consistency. Remove from heat. Transfer to a glass bowl and refrigerate for several hours to thicken. You can fish out the star anise now or later, just don't let it end up in the cookies.

Preheat oven to 350 degrees.

On a floured board, roll out the cookie dough to ¼ inch thick. Cut out circles using a cookie cutter or the mouth of a glass. Place a spoonful of filling in the middle of the circle. Fold in the sides to form a triangle shape, pinching or crimping the edges.

Transfer to a lightly greased cookie sheet. Bake for about 20 minutes until golden.

Special note: Invariably, you will find yourself with more dough than filling. This is a good problem to have! You can fill the rest with traditional ingredients, like apricot, prune, or raspberry preserves. Or go crazy and try it with Nutella or peanut butter.

Masala Popcorn

his one is so easy, it hardly counts as a recipe. All you need are the right (two) ingredients. If you're using microwave popcorn, opt for a low-salt or no-salt variety since the chaat masala already has a ton of it.

4 cups of popped popcorn
1 tablespoon chaat masala powder

Place popcorn in a large bowl and sprinkle chaat masala on top. Toss to coat evenly. Eat. Lick fingers. Repeat.

Paula J. Freedman

has another career in digital media, in which she has made websites for a well-known children's publisher, a TV network, and assorted others. She studied publishing at Pace University and English at the State University of New York at Buffalo. In addition to writing fiction, Paula enjoys reading, traveling, and knitting. She lives with her husband and two parrots in New York City. *My Basmati Bat Mitzvah* is her first book.

LIKED THIS BOOK?

CHECK OUT THESE OTHER GREAT READS!

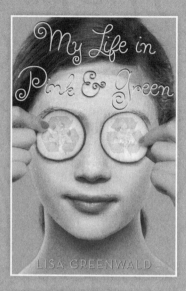

SEND AUTHOR FAN MAIL TO:
Amulet Books, Attn: Marketing, 115 West 18th Street, New York, NY 10011.
Or e-mail marketing@abramsbooks.com. All mail will be forwarded.

Amulet Books
An imprint of ABRAMS
WWW.AMULETBOOKS.COM